# WORLD CUP FEVER

A FANATIC'S GUIDE TO THE STARS,
TEAMS, STORIES, CONTROVERSY,
AND EXCITEMENT OF SPORTS'
GREATEST EVENT

## STEPHEN REA

D0452049

Skyhorse Publishing

Skyhorse Publishing books may be purchased in bulk at special discounts for sales promotion, corporate gifts, fund-raising, or educational purposes. Special editions can also be created to specifications. For details, contact the Special Sales Department, Skyhorse Publishing, 307 West 36th Street, 11th Floor, New York, NY 10018 or info@skyhorsepublishing.com.

Skyhorse® and Skyhorse Publishing® is are registered trademarks of Skyhorse Publishing, Inc.®, a Delaware corporation.

Visit our website at www.skyhorsepublishing.com.

10 9 8 7 6 5 4 3 2 1

Library of Congress Cataloging-in-Publication Data is available on file.

Cover design by Tom Lau
Cover photos courtesy of Associated Press
All interior photos courtesy of Associated Press, unless otherwise noted.

Print ISBN: 978-1-5107-1808-1
Ebook ISBN: 978-1-5107-1809-8

Printed in the United States of America

This book is dedicated to my daughter Nicola.
Every day you bring me more joy than Northern Ireland's
win over Spain at the 1982 World Cup.

# CONTENTS

# PREFACE: BIRTH OF A FAN

I USED TO CALL IT "football." Now I call it "soccer." Sometimes I call it "football" in the States which confuses Americans. Sometimes I call it "soccer" in the UK and I get accused of turning into a Yank.

I was born in Belfast, Northern Ireland, in 1969, the same year that what we euphemistically call "The Troubles" started. The two events are not related. My dad was still thirty-eight days short of his twenties when I arrived, and I'm sure an unplanned baby boy fitted into his packed soccer-playing and watching schedule just dandy. My love of the sport comes from him, though my mum said I wasn't interested in kicking a ball at first and he was crestfallen. He used to ask her what was wrong with me.

We lived in a tiny two-up, two-down house off the hardscrabble Newtownards Road. I grew up with paramilitary roadblocks, civilian murders, and soldiers patrolling the streets. Our tiny terraced home was burgled and my parents wanted the biggest dog they could find as a deterrent, and the bundle of fur we brought home exploded into a gigantic, but docile St. Bernard we needed to walk in the park. My dad fell into the habit of bringing along a ball, I kicked it with him, and according to my mum that's when I found soccer: my passion spawned from the matrimony of an intimidating, but useless guard dog and the fear of sectarian criminality.

It says a lot that in my family, getting into soccer when I was a four-year-old toddler is considered coming to the sport late.

But late convert that I was, soon I too was in love with the beautiful game.

One Christmas in the mid-seventies, my parents gave me a Chelsea kit. To this day I don't know why my dad bought it for me as he was a Manchester United fan who worshiped George Best (the only jersey I'd ever get for my child would be Chelsea and I'd rather drown them in the bath than see them wear red. That's why my daughter grew up hating Santa Claus—I'm like a particularly violent and hardcore reincarnation of Senator Joseph McCarthy). I keep meaning to ask my dad why he bought a Chelsea outfit but I know he won't remember anyway. My guess is it was cheap. That's how they became my team and I was condemned to decades of misery.

Today the Blues are one of the most popular and successful clubs in the world, but for the majority of the seventies and eighties we were rubbish, yo-yoing between the top two divisions in England. It was so unusual to support them back then that some friends nicknamed me "Chelsea." My mate Brian White was the only other Chelsea fan I even knew, and we remain close today. We share an unbreakable bond of hardship, just like Vietnam vets.

I was nine when I first got to see Chelsea in person. My mum took me to London in March 1979 for a match against Liverpool, then the reigning European champions. We were relegated that year from the top flight (see, told you we were rubbish) but we played really well and held them to a scoreless draw. I felt like a real fan. We went twenty-six years without winning a trophy but I wouldn't swap it for the world.

The good news was I passed an exam that won me free tuition at a private all-boys school. The bad news was they played rugby, not soccer. Soccer was seen as a working-class folly watched by hooligans, while rugby was the refined British endeavor for gentlemen, so I played in streets and parks and leisure centers. However, that education led to a journalism job on a national newspaper in England, and I frequently followed Chelsea both home and away in the days when you could just show up and pay at the turnstile.

Then in a barely believable left-field career lurch I returned to Northern Ireland in the nineties and bought the travel agency next door to my dad's small commercial printing business. Dangerously armed with a direct link into airline and hotel reservation systems, I was like an unstable megalomaniac, able to book trips anywhere in the world with Chelsea and the Northern Ireland national team, even jetting off to places like Belarus and Lithuania on a whim to watch their Under-16 squads.

In a split second that changed my life, in December 1995 in a London bar the night before Ozzy Osbourne's birthday party (seriously), I met a girl from North Carolina who handed me her number. How different things would be if she had not done that, or I had drunkenly lost the slip of paper. Five years later we married, four years after that we moved to the States, within a decade we owned a house in New Orleans and were battered by Hurricane Katrina.

I have now lived in Louisiana for fourteen years and experienced firsthand the USA's embrace of soccer. Not fully, not totally, not yet offered the imported brandy or a few pieces of the fancy Belgian chocolate at Christmas. But it is no longer the redheaded stepchild of sports, banished to eat in the kids' playroom when it visits for Thanksgiving and left out of the family reunion at the beach. The game is inexorably, inevitably, incontrovertibly whee-dling its way into the nation's affection.

I helped form a team based at an Irish bar and wrote a book about that, and what it was like to go through Katrina, titled, *Finn McCool's Football Club: The Birth, Death, and Resurrection of a Pub Soccer Team in the City of the Dead*. A media guy at Chelsea read it and asked me to write a weekly column for their website entitled, *A Blogger from America*. From a nine-year-old Irish nipper at his first Blues game to a middle-aged American citizen working for the club. All because of my behemoth childhood dog, Susie.

And so to this book, written to tie in with the USA's appearance at Russia 2018. That will teach me.

"Of course the States will be at the World Cup, they haven't missed out in more than thirty years!" I confidently predicted to everyone, right up until the last qualifier. The luck of the Irish, my arse.

But don't let the United States' absence put you off the tournament. I guarantee it will still offer tragedy and triumph and every conceivable emotion in between. It's still the beautiful game. And it's still the greatest sporting event in the world.

# INTRODUCTION

I'VE ALWAYS LOVED THE WORLD Cup. The affair is four decades old.

The first soccer match I ever saw was a World Cup qualifier on October 12, 1977, between Northern Ireland and Holland. I was seven. Two true legends, Irishman George Best and the Netherland's Johann Cruyff, played that day. A pair to grace any all-time dream team, a couple of attackers both crowned European Player of the Year—and they were on the same field for my first professional contest. It was all downhill from there, right?

Cruyff captained Holland at the 1974 World Cup, the team many consider the greatest to have never won the tournament, but he pulled out of playing for the 1978 squad. Best died in 2005, having never made the finals. Both went on to star in the North American Soccer League (NASL).

But let's focus on that wee Irish lad, sniveling and shivering on the crumbling terraces of Windsor Park, Belfast, in the seventies in Ulster, a dark time in my country's history defined by explosions, car bombs, and sectarian murder. Games were played in the afternoon then rather than at night because of the pervading threat of civil unrest, with kids sprung from school and adults sneaking out of work to watch their national team. I would love to write that it was the day that changed my life, the moment I decided to become a football writer, that forty years later I still remember the riot of color of the flags and the din of the crowd's songs and the cloying smell of frying onions and the roughness of the rusted crash barrier against my unblemished childish hand.

But I can't. I don't remember what I felt.

I recall one solitary detail: my dad telling a friend he was only there to see Best. Why such a throwaway remark remains lodged in my brain I can't say. But that's it. The sum total of my memory from the ninety minutes two soccer superstars strutted their stuff just feet away.

The finals the following year were in Argentina, an exotic dangerous destination with a ruling military junta, and the late-night kickoffs put most games beyond the reach of this eight-year-old. But I have vivid recollections from that June. I watched the flickering wavy pictures as Scotland, Britain's sole representative, was destroyed by a Teófilo Cubillas-inspired Peru, an indelible image seared into my brain as he skipped through the Jocks' defense wearing that iconic white uniform with the red slash.

The Scots then embarrassingly tied 1–1 with Iran, winger John Robertson was sent home for failing a drug test, and coach Ally MacLeod told reporters at their training ground as he bent to pet a dog, "This is the only friend I have left." The dog bit him.

Scotland needed to beat the Dutch by three clear goals to make the second round, and after a brilliant individual goal from pint-size midfield dynamo Archie Gemmill (since immortalized in the movie *Trainspotting*) they were 3–1 ahead, but Holland pulled a goal back and sent the Tartan Army packing to drown their sorrows in their whiskey.

Though it was a school night, I had been allowed to stay up late to watch the contest, and afterwards I laid in bed in our small suburban bungalow and dictated notes to my mum for my dad so he had a recap of the match when he came home from drumming in a cover band.

It was a captivating tournament and pivotal for me. The sky blue and white strips of the host nation's shirts and the ticker tape and the kaleidoscopic fans combining for a Technicolor sporting experience which permanently etched the World Cup into my head, into my body, into my psyche.

But if I thought the 1978 World Cup was special, the next edition was something else. I was there.

Northern Irish soccer had enjoyed a resurgence under coach Billy Bingham, but after being lumped into a strong qualifying group with Scotland, Sweden, Portugal, and Israel (a section thus stretching from the Middle East to the last spit of land before you reached America), no one but the craziest Ulsterman—and to be fair we had plenty as we continued to rip our country apart during The Troubles—expected us to make the finals.

But all five nations were more evenly matched than anyone expected, and the defining moment of the campaign came on October 15, 1981, as my dad and I listened to the 8 a.m. local news on the radio in our kitchen in Dundonald.

When the bulletin reached the sports section, I distinctly recall the female presenter's words: "Northern Ireland's hopes of qualifying for the World Cup were given a boost last night when Sweden beat Portugal, 2–1." My dad and I roared with delight then went back to our tea and toast. If we had been American we would probably have high-fived and wolfed down our waffles.

We defeated Israel, 1–0, the following month and our tiny country of 1.5 million made the big time for only our second appearance ever and our first since 1958. We headed for Spain.

I don't think there was a discussion about taking me out of school for two weeks and missing important exams to watch soccer. I do remember taking a list of homework from each teacher, textbooks and tests for me to work on at our stultifying, sun-battered vacation apartment on the Costa del Sol (my English teacher was a soccer fan and thirty-six years later I still remember his succinct instructions: "Keep reading!"). I don't know if I did much studying about Charlemagne and the Holy Roman Empire, but I definitely played and watched tons of soccer, and swam a

My cousin David, me, and my dad Billy at the 1982 World Cup before Northern Ireland played Yugoslavia to a 0–0 tie in Zaragoza, Spain. *From the author's collection.*

lot (If my daughter is reading this, then I was always a straight-A student and studied *a lot*).

The three greatest words in the English language: "I was there." I was there for the greatest night in the history of the Irish Football Association.

After tying both Yugoslavia and Honduras, we had to defeat host nation Spain in the cauldron of Valencia to make the next round. No one gave us a chance. The squad packed up and checked out of the hotel before the game. We were outside the stadium when their team bus crawled up at a snail's pace, negotiating through the cacophonous crowd chanting and blowing whistles. A spine-tingling, charged, electric atmosphere, as the part-time

A view from the terrace in the Luis Casanova Stadium in Valencia, June 25, 1982. Little Northern Ireland, down to ten men, were about to beat the hosts Spain 1-0. *From the author's collection.*

Irish League players on the bus snapped photos and my dad told me, "If you are gonna go out of the World Cup then you wanna go out like this."

But we didn't go out. We won. Against all the odds, and despite having a player sent off after an hour, we beat Spain, 1–0. We defeated the hosts to win the group and advanced to the second stage. Writing about it today still gives me chills and goose bumps even in Louisiana's steamy sultry summer.

I don't remember much from the match, though I recall the aftermath: climbing onto the fence surrounding the field and shaking hands with defender John McCelland, walking through the streets of Valencia as locals clapped us, the sing-song on the journey back to our base.

We then tied with Austria, 2–2, and in what was effectively a playoff for a semi-final spot we lost to a ferociously talented French team, 4–1. I was in the crowd that thronged the streets when the squad paraded through Belfast on an open-top bus that November, and the following day we beat European Champions and World Cup finalists West Germany, 1–0. We had a helluva team back then.

Italy won the final, 3–1, but ask any soccer fan my age about that game and what they will remember is Marco Tardelli's celebration after scoring the second goal. His face, an expression of intense ecstasy as he yells a primeval, primordial scream while running, arms flailing, fists pumping. When I think about the passion and pleasure soccer can bring, it's his expression I conjure up.

Four years later, the tournament sashayed to Mexico and guess what? Northern Ireland made it again! No appearances for twenty-four years and then two in succession, like a particularly obstreperous and contrary hardcore bus company.

Our qualifying group contained England, Romania, Turkey, and Finland. I went to Finland to watch us start with a disastrous defeat in Pori, a sleepy seaside village better suited to hosting a summer church fete than an important sporting event. Results waxed and waned and our final two matches were our hardest challenges on the road in Romania and England.

We booked a week's vacation package with the Northern Ireland fans to Bulgaria with a day-trip to Bucharest for the match. Eastern Europe in October during the 1980s was worse than you can imagine. Absolutely nothing—I mean really, truly, literally nothing—to see or do. We tried to find a flight home three days early. The presents we brought home for my cousins were chestnuts we found on the ground for them to play conkers with, which illustrates the variety of shopping available.

However, soccer-wise, it was exciting and beautiful and wonderful because we beat Romania, 1–0. We scored after 29 minutes, then spent the next hour defending for our lives without ever crossing the halfway line, and the following month we secured a scoreless tie with England and a spot at the 1986 tournament.

But I couldn't go. At sixteen, and in the middle of important national exams, I wasn't getting away this time. My dad went while I watched on TV through a heavy haze of sweat and acne cream. It was more late-night kickoffs but my exam schedule meant I didn't have to be at school every day. We had a static fitness bike and I set it in front of the TV, peddling furiously for a hormone-ravaged month as I fought to get lean and supple and thus attractive to girls.

In our opener we tied with Algeria, 1–1, (thirty-one years later in a downtown hotel in Houston, our goalscorer, Norman Whiteside, showed me the watch he received from FIFA for that sixth-minute goal as one of the ten fastest in the competition), then we were unlucky to lose, 2–1, to Spain. We bowed out with a 3–0 defeat to Brazil, and more than three decades later, I still hear stories from Irish fans about this tournament.

By 1990, I was an adult and let loose in the real world. I had won a job on the biggest-selling English-language daily newspaper on the planet and they whisked me to the British mainland. I sped through an accelerated journalism program and was lodging with a family on the outskirts of Manchester.

The Republic of Ireland had qualified and my English landlord (in a move that may resonate with some Americans) adopted them as his team. Apparently three generations back he had Irish heritage, or he had once drank a pint of Guinness . . . anyway, something tenuous. My Northern Irish girlfriend was at college seventy miles away in Birmingham and I usually spent three nights a week with her. I can admit now this was not motivated solely by young love but was also to escape my increasingly bizarre housing situation.

The family of four who owned the house was strapped for cash after the father lost his job. He found solace—surprise, surprise—in heavy drinking. So they took in more and more lodgers, including many overseas students who spoke little or no English, and as his drinking worsened, and the tenants multiplied, the downward spiral caused the couple to split.

But they couldn't afford to physically separate, so the wife set up a makeshift camp-bed under the stairs like a doughy female middle-aged Harry Potter, only in an alcove, not a cupboard. Her "room" didn't have a door. The tension swirling through the home meant mealtimes were a laugh-fest, the father often passing out drunk, face-down in his rice or trying to eat soup with a fork.

In 1994 the USA hosted the World Cup. Every European soccer expert agreed it was madness to award the tournament to the Yanks and many thought it was the first sign of the apocalypse. But it was a great success, and not just because of the USA's patriotic shirts and Alexi Lalas's beard.

It was the second tournament I went to. I had left journalism and was now a travel agent in Belfast, and after dating a Northern Irish girl while I lived in England I was now dating an English girl while I lived in Northern Ireland.

We road-tripped for five weeks from LA through the southern states to DC and caught the semifinal between Brazil and Sweden at the Rose Bowl in Pasadena. We went in a stretch limo with Ozzy Osbourne's personal assistant Tony, his office manager Michael, and his son Jack. But that's a story for another book.

It was a tedious game, the most memorable thing the unbearable lack of shade in the stands, and a few days later I returned as organizers gave away free tickets to the third-place playoff (the local paper ran an article about how America only likes winners so no one wanted to watch the losing semifinalists Sweden and Bulgaria play).

On the day of the final between Italy and Brazil I got up early to trawl the paper's classifieds and called dozens of scalpers looking for a ticket (that's what you did before online resale sites). All were hundreds of dollars, and although I knew it could be my only chance to watch a World Cup final, I couldn't justify pulling the trigger on such a large amount. So I watched the lifeless championship match alongside Michael, with whom I was staying. Importantly, it was the first time I ever had chips and salsa.

By France in 1998 I had bought a cozy seafront apartment that—totally coincidentally but joyfully—happened to be joined to a pleasant pub. That summer, my friends flocked over to watch matches at my place and then we would migrate next door. Sometimes we would meet in the bar then head back to mine after. Sometimes we would bounce back and forth. It was every bit as magical as it sounds.

Then things changed, both in my life and with the World Cup. It's hard to say which was the more seismic.

I had married an American. I was determined to make my love life as complicated and as geographically challenged as possible. Her deep-seated hatred of soccer led me to send her home to North Carolina for a month in 2002. Never one to miss a trick, I got publicity for my travel agency and sold the story to the papers (It ran in one with the headline, "I packed my wife off so I could watch the Cup in peace").

With Japan and Korea co-hosting the tournament it caused bleary-eyed early kickoffs for us in Europe, so if you wanted to watch every match—and trust me, I did—it required creative planning. I brought a portable TV into my office and hid it behind the door so it was invisible from the store, and I spent a month pretending to attend to important travel business while my harried, pressurized employees dealt with customers. I had them schedule their lunch breaks and doctor appointments around vital events like China vs. Costa Rica. I took them all out to dinner to thank them for putting up with me—after the tournament ended, obviously.

Next I moved continents—just in time to be hit by the most destructive natural disaster to ever hit the United States.

My wife missed her family, missed the sun, missed shop assistants telling her to have a nice day rather than hide in the back watching soccer. In July 2004 we moved to New Orleans, Louisiana, and the following February we bought a house in the area called Uptown. Six months later, Hurricane Katrina slammed into us, broke the levees, and flooded 80 percent of the city.

The Big Easy's soccer bar Finn McCool's Irish Pub was devastated, the Mid-City neighborhood drowned under eight feet of water. It reopened on St Patrick's Day 2006 so it had only been back in business ten weeks when the World Cup in Germany rolled around.

No traffic lights, the vast majority of homes uninhabited, dumpsters full of rotting wood and mushed drywall scattered on the streets, abandoned and encrusted vehicles flecking the roads. Finn's was gutted and rebuilt but there was still a high-water line marked halfway up the windows. The aftershocks and day-to-day challenges of living in a city slowly and painfully coming back to life were with us all everywhere, every day. At a time when simple errands like mailing a letter could take hours (few post offices were operating and they had such long lines they were managed by the police), a visit to Finn's to watch soccer was a welcome and much-needed distraction.

It was frequently jammed, a gumbo mix of nationalities and a myriad of supporters from around the globe who created a vibrant, diverse, pulsing mass of humanity. When you've been forced to abandon your home, when you have returned to find everything you have ever owned swept away, when you have been washed out of your job, when you've had to reconstruct your life and start again . . . a month watching the World Cup is extremely cathartic, trust me.

Four years later, the World Cup went to South Africa and although New Orleans was almost back to its old dysfunctional self, life had changed for me. I was now a father. My daughter, Nicola, was born in July 2007 and I was a stay-at-home dad. It cramped my soccer-watching-at-the-pub lifestyle.

Instead I was forced to follow matches at home between hosting teddy bear tea parties, playing with dolls, and settling arguments between Panda and Ladybug. Nicola was coming out of the terrible twos and entering the even-bloody-worse-that-nobody-tells-you-about threes, an only child used to constant stimulation and attention. Trying to watch Australia play Ghana while simultaneously having my nails painted and adjusting my tiara was a challenge, but one I successfully managed.

I became an expert on Disney princesses, glitter, and what cleans milk stains from your couch when your attention wanders from your toddler while engrossed in Slovakia and New Zealand. It was a tournament of learning, parenting, and planning trips to the children's museum or library story times around the vagaries of kickoffs in Cape Town and Johannesburg. And event planners who put on the Democratic and Republican conventions think they have it tough.

Occasionally—and by that I mean all day Saturday and Sunday—I went to Finn's. The Americans took on England in the first round, and the local USA supporters club The Bayou Militia had been on a recruiting spree like a Russian billionaire buying a Premier League club. The English fans, most of whom were regulars before Hurricane Katrina, hired a luxury minibus and parked it outside so they could watch the match (in a van, in the street) in comfort. It ended 1–1 so everyone went home happy (apart from the English, who thought that a tie with the USA was a national catastrophe).

The final between Holland and Spain was also a memorable day. Louisiana summers are oppressively overpowering, the energy-sapping soaring temperatures only counter-weighted by sky-cracking thunderstorms bringing torrential downpours and deafening thunder, submerging the sidewalks beneath a blanket of black.

The pub was struck by lightning in the second half and it knocked out the satellite system. The power died as well and sweat steamed off smelly soccer shirts like a fat man who had run a marathon inside a Turkish bath.

My friend Paul streamed the game on his phone and we huddled like marooned Arctic explorers as we tried to follow the contest on a two-inch screen. Then inspiration struck (just as the lightning had), and I called my friend Mary on the next block to discover she still had electricity. I shouted, "C'mon everybody!" (probably in an Eddie Cochran voice, my memory is hazy) and we splashed and waded through the puddles, invading her front room to watch the rest of the final. We soaked her carpets and drenched her furniture and drank all her beer, then we thanked her and left, lamenting it would be another four years before we could do it all again.

And that brings me to Brazil, 2014. Nicola had just finished first grade, and in a disappointing non-break from tradition, this World Cup was held at exactly the same time as every other World Cup and took place while she was on summer vacation. So it was my job to look after her.

Once again it was watching matches between board games and negotiating with her to let me see Honduras play Switzerland for an hour of Scooby Doo, dragging her out of bed to go to the park so we would be back in time for games, turning down playdates and invites to go with her friends to the zoo she never even knew about so I could concentrate on Iran's match with Nigeria.

By now, the World Cup was mainstream and The Bayou Militia had mutated into a full-fledged army with banners and flags and scarves and tanks . . . not really, but it seemed like it. At Finn's for the first USA match against Ghana they needed crash barriers to corral the legion of Stars and Stripes-waving patriots in love with the beautiful game. Welcome to prime time.

So that's my World Cup love story.

I look back on growing up and growing old and define stages of my life by the host country, memorable images, and unforgettable moments from the greatest sporting event on Earth. An eight-year-old curled up on the carpet in front of late-night TV in

Me with legendary Northern Irish goalkeeper Pat Jennings at the team's hotel the night before they defeated hosts Spain at the 1982 World Cup. *From the author's collection.*

Belfast watching the cascading ticker tape float down and flutter onto the field in Buenos Aires. The prepubescent boy who knew Marco Tardelli's screaming, fist-waving celebration in Spain would be stamped into his mind forever. Paul Gascoigne's tears at Italia '90 as I started my work career in his England. David Beckham's redemption against Argentina in faraway Asia as I juggled following the game with taking care of my travel agency clients. Gasping as the Germans destroyed the Samba Boys in their own backyard while I completed a jigsaw puzzle with my daughter.

From a little boy marveling at exotic faraway images to a father living on another continent, the World Cup has always been, and continues to be, the constant background to my life. Maybe one day you will feel the same way. Enjoy.

# CHAPTER 1

# THE STORY OF THE WORLD CUP

## 1930 Uruguay

Every four years more than 200 countries, including tiny Pacific islands and mountainous Asian nations and sandstorm-battered lands in Africa, compete to appear on the biggest sporting stage on earth. But only a dozen teams in the whole world traveled to join the hosts for the first World Cup in July 1930.

Scotland had played England as far back as 1870, three decades later the first international outside Britain was a clash between Austria and Hungary (history buffs insert your own joke about the Austro-Hungarian Empire and the Habsburg Monarchy), and in Paris in 1904, the Fédération Internationale de Football Association (FIFA) was born with seven members: France, Belgium, Denmark, Netherlands, Spain, Sweden, and Switzerland. The British joined the following year but withdrew after World War I, refusing to play any countries they had been at war with and then extending the boycott to include any nations which had competed against former enemies. They rejoined in the 1920s, then withdrew again in a dispute about the definition of amateurism and stayed out until after World War II. And you thought Brexit was a recent phenomenon.

In 1928, FIFA set up a world championship and commissioned a gold trophy, later named after their president, Jules Rimet, and five European countries offered to host it. So, of course, it was awarded to Uruguay, who were reigning Olympic champions and celebrating a century of independence. The clincher was they offered to pay the expenses of every European country, though it turned out to be a cheap date as only four bothered to make the two-week-long sea voyage to Montevideo. All the snubbed hosts huffed and refused to attend—Europeans were particularly touchy back then and quick to take offense. Not much has changed.

Eight weeks out not a single European nation had entered, and the insulted South American countries threatened to withdraw from FIFA (if you were involved in soccer administration back then you spent your time placating touchy nations). An embarrassed Rimet eventually strong-armed Belgium, France, Romania, and Yugoslavia into signing on along with the USA, Mexico, and seven South American teams.

Four shared the same ship in what was the most complicated and longest ride-share in history. The Romanians boarded in Italy, called for the French, picked up the Belgians in Spain, then stopped for the Brazilians in Rio. Rimet threw the trophy in his hand luggage and jumped aboard as well.

The first stage was made up of four groups, three containing three teams and one with four, the winners of each section advancing to the semifinal. Presciently, the World Cup was embroiled in controversy within 48 hours of its birth.

France were 1–0 down to Argentina with their striker clean through on goal when the Brazilian referee blew for full-time.

Unfortunately there was still six minutes to play. After a bit of pushing and shoving and an appearance by the mounted police, the official apologized and the game resumed but France failed to find the equalizer. Their captain, Alexandre Villaplane, was shot in 1944 by the Resistance for collaborating with the Nazis.

The Argentinians won all three games even though their captain, Manuel Ferreira, missed the second contest against Mexico because he literally "jumped ship" and sailed back across the River Plate to take a law exam. They beat the USA, 6–1, in the semifinal.

Uruguay defeated Peru, 1–0, one hundred years to the very day since the creation of the country's constitution: this was due to accident rather than design, the scheduling had been thrown off because the new Estadio Centenario stadium (the largest outside Britain) built for the finals was not ready in time. They, too, won their last-four contest, 6–1, against Yugoslavia, made up solely of Serbs as the Croats were boycotting the national team.

And so to the first World Cup final, a repeat of the 1928 Olympic decider and bizarrely scheduled for a 2 p.m. kickoff on a Wednesday.

As tens of thousands of Argentinians scrambled to cross the river in scenes resembling the World War II evacuation at Dunkirk, a row erupted with both sides insisting their ball should be used. They agreed to play one half with each: which one was the rounder has been lost to the mists of time. The Belgian referee refused to take the field until his safety was assured and insisted on having a boat ready at the harbor, presumably with the engine running in case he needed a quick getaway.

The hosts roared into an early lead thanks to Pablo Dorado but the visitors leveled through Carlos Peucelle, then tournament top scorer Guillermo Stábile's eighth strike put them ahead. But by halfway through the second half Uruguay were back in front courtesy of Pedro Cea and Santos Iriarte, and with a minute to go Héctor Castro (who was missing the lower part of his left arm) hit the fourth. Uruguay added the World Cup to their two Olympic titles and the host nation declared a national holiday, while in the Argentinian capital they attacked the Uruguayan embassy.

The World Cup was up and running. Once every four years a month in my summer would never be the same again.

Uruguay's Pablo Dorado scores the first-ever World Cup final goal, Montevideo, Uruguay, July 30, 1930.

## 1934 Italy

The only World Cup in which the champions did not defend their title. Uruguay, like Achilles sulking in his tent during the Trojan War, stayed at home in protest of so few Europeans coming to their party. It's also the only time the hosts had to win a qualifier to play in their own tournament, Italy safely negotiating a playoff against Greece.

But after whittling the thirty-six applicants down to sixteen nations, FIFA turned the World Cup into a single elimination event from the get-go. Egypt, the first Africans to appear at the finals, went all the way to Naples, conceded four times to Hungary, and then disappeared from the tournament for the next fifty-six years. All four non-European nations were knocked out immediately, weeks of preparation and travel for an hour-and-a-half's action. The eight first-round matches took place simultaneously so less than two hours after kicking off we had reached the quarterfinals.

The last eight saw the first replay ever, the hosts squeaking past Spain, 1–0, the day after a violent 1–1 tie in which the Italian Mario Pizziolo suffered such a bad leg break he never played for the national team again. He eventually received a World Cup winner's medal in 1988, fifty-four years after the win and two years before he died.

Italy then beat the fabled Austrians known as the Wunderteam on a churned field in a torrential downpour in Milan, and in the final lined up against Czechoslovakia, who had seen off Germany (German Sigi Haringer was dropped for the third-place playoff by the disciplinarian coach Otto Nerz for the heinous crime of eating an orange at a train station).

The decider was held in Rome on June 10 in a temperature of more than 100 degrees. The militaristic way the teams parade onto the field, the fans in uniform on the terraces, fascist dictator Benito Mussolini in the stands . . . it's impossible not to view the footage today through the awful hindsight of knowing the horrors to come by the end of the decade.

Antonín Puč put the Czechs ahead with 19 minutes to go, but Raimundo Orsi equalized with a freakish curling shot—the next day he tried to repeat it for photographers but gave up after twenty attempts—and we had the first final to go to extra time. Italian Angelo Schiavio hit the winner and the home fans joined their pot-bellied leader in celebration.

## 1938 France

If the jackboot of fascism was hovering over the soccer world in 1934, four years later it had stomped down and crushed the game's neck. The planet was on the brink of being plunged into history's most blood-curdling conflict, and within two years the Germans had invaded and occupied the host country.

It had been assumed the tournament would alternate between continents but Frenchman Jules Rimet, FIFA president for more than three decades by now, secured it for his home country instead. Guess what happened? Uruguay and Argentina boycotted it in protest. However, despite thirty-seven entrants, FIFA still found themselves a finalist short. The ineptitude of the men tasked with running the world's most popular sport in the 1930s is staggering.

Austria had qualified for the World Cup but after the Anschluss, when Nazi Germany annexed the country, the independent nation no longer existed, (Five Austrians started for Germany against Switzerland, and after they lost after a replay the coach blamed the Austrians. It's the only time Germany has failed to reach the quarterfinals.)

Rather than have another country replace Austria, they awarded their scheduled opponents Sweden a walkover into the last eight. The Swedes smashed Cuba, 8–0, and were thus in the semifinal after playing just one mismatched game. Meanwhile, the Dutch East Indies (now Indonesia) were trounced, 6–0, by Hungary but earned a place in history as the only nation to have played just one game at a World Cup.

Champions Italy were on a 19-game unbeaten run when they came up against the hosts in the quarterfinal. Despite their nickname being the Azzurri because of their blue uniforms, at Mussolini's insistence they played in black shirts to mimic the dress of his totalitarian thugs. They beat France, 3–1, to set up a semifinal with an overconfident Brazil who rested their star Leônidas, The Black Diamond (who had scored a tournament-best seven goals), for the final and lost, 2–1.

It was Italy against Hungary, who had thrashed the lucky Swedes, 5–1, in the semifinal, in the championship game. It was rumored Mussolini sent a telegram to the Italians warning that if they didn't win he would have them executed. After Italy lifted the trophy, the Hungarian goalkeeper, Antal Szabó, was reported to have said, "I may have let in four goals, but at least I saved the lives of eleven men." Years later, however, the team said Il Duce had simply sent a note wishing them luck.

After a pregame fascist straight-arm salute to their leader, Gino Colaussi opened the scoring, but almost straight from the restart Pál Titkos equalized. However, Silvio Piola restored Italy's lead and then Colaussi's second strike gave them a 3–1 cushion at the half. György Sárosi made it 3–2, but Piola's second goal made it safe—Italy remain the only team to have won the World Cup twice under the same coach, Vittorio Pozzo.

The trophy spent World War II hidden in a shoebox under the bed of Italian FIFA vice president Ottorino Barassi. It would be a dozen years before the next global reunion.

# 1950 Brazil

World War II canceled both the 1942 and 1946 editions, so by 1950 everyone had forgotten who was mad with whom, and no one could remember whose turn it was to boycott the competition, so everybody stayed away just to be sure. No, not really, though Argentina withdrew again over some perceived slight by the Brazilian hosts. Also, Germany and Japan were on the naughty step and banned from taking part, disappointing the fugitive Nazis hiding in South America who were hoping to see the Fatherland.

After two straight knockout tournaments the World Cup reverted to featuring sixteen teams in four groups of four. But just like twenty years previous, only thirteen bothered to show up.

The British championship featuring England, Scotland, Northern Ireland, and Wales was a qualifying group with the top two making the finals. To prove they were as arrogant as their southern neighbors, Scotland declared they would only travel to Brazil as British champions. They lost at home to England, finished as runners-up, and sat at home pouting.

An apocryphal piece of soccer trivia is that India made this World Cup but refused to compete when FIFA banned them from playing in bare feet. While they did play barefoot in the 1948 Olympics, they actually withdrew because of the expenses involved in an 18,000-mile round-trip. They remain the only country to have qualified for the World Cup but who have not played a finals game.

With a symmetrical first-stage shot, you might guess that FIFA rearranged the groups into three sections of three and one of four as they had in 1930. Of course not—they kept the original groups even after the withdrawals, with the lopsided result that two groups had four teams, one had three, and one had two. In Group 4, Uruguay blew out Bolivia, 8–0, to make the final round.

Italy, the two-time champions, had sailed to the competition in a draining weeks-long odyssey rather than fly, their national psyche scarred by the Superga air disaster that had wiped out the Torino club a year earlier. Sweden handed them their first-ever World Cup defeat and qualified for the next stage, Spain joined them after defeating the USA, Chile, and England (still reeling from their loss to the USA three days earlier). Hosts Brazil made up the quartet after beating Yugoslavia, the Slavs handicapped by temporarily playing a man short as Rajko Mitic had banged his head and cut it open on the walk from the dressing room to the field!

This was the only World Cup without a championship match. Brazil had insisted two round-robin stages made better financial sense with more games and more spectators: the average attendance of more than 60,000 was a record that stood until the event came to the US forty-four years later. In the final round the hosts caught fire, rattling seven past Sweden and six past Spain. Meanwhile, Uruguay stumbled and bumbled in their wake, needing a late equalizer to tie Spain, 2–2, and then an even later winner to squeeze past Sweden, 3–2.

But the showdown between the South Americans (a de-facto final) produced a result so shocking it spawned a term, *Maracanazo* (the Maracana blow) still used today. Uruguay beat Brazil, 2–1, and were crowned World Champions for a second time.

# 1954 Switzerland

By the fifth incarnation twenty-four years after the inaugural competition, you might think FIFA had finally settled on a format. You would be wrong.

Having had a round-robin group stage followed by semifinals, then straight knockout eliminations, then a round-robin first stage followed by another round-robin stage, they tinkered once more. They again started with four groups of four but seeded two teams in each, proclaiming that the seeds only had to play the other two non-seeds. So each section had four countries but each only played two games. What purpose this served is unclear, I assume it was a fudged, botched halfway-house between a straight knockout competition and a group stage guaranteeing everyone three games. It didn't make any sense.

For the first time South Americans had to play qualifiers (previously countries just withdrew or sulked in a corner), though you will be astonished to read that Argentina were unhappy about something or other and refused to take part for the third successive tournament.

Meanwhile, Europe saw its first major qualification shock with Spain, fourth in 1950, failing to make it. They beat Turkey at home, lost to them away, and tied 2–2 in a playoff in Rome. So, the fourteen-year-old son of a stadium worker was blindfolded and picked Turkey's name out of the hat. That was how you made it to the World Cup in the 1950s—it would be almost half a century before the Turks qualified again.

It left FIFA with a problem as Spain were one of the eight seeds. As they had three months to rectify the situation a gentle rejig of the rankings would probably have been in order, but they elected not to. They gave Spain's seeding to Turkey who were promptly hammered, 4–1, by the unseeded West Germans, the new country created as Germany was cleaved in two by the rise of the Iron Curtain across Europe.

The counterintuitive nature of this tournament continued into the knockout stages, with the four group winners placed in one half of the draw and the four runners-up in the other, guaranteeing one would be in the final. In the "second-place" bracket the ding-dong contest between the hosts and Austria is the highest-scoring match in World Cup history. It saw *nine* goals in the first 39 minutes, the Austrians ahead 5–4 at halftime and finally running out 7–5 winners. Players on both sides notched hat tricks (Theodor Wagner for Austria and Sepp Huegi for Switzerland).

Meanwhile, the quarterfinal between Brazil and Hungary, The Battle of Berne, would live in infamy. A penalty awarded to Hungary by English referee Arthur Ellis sparked a field invasion by Brazilian staff, substitutes, and even reporters, all of whom had to be marched off by police. The remaining half-an-hour was a stream of cynical challenges and increasingly violent fouls degenerating into all-out attacks. One player from each team were sent off for fighting, another Brazilian was dismissed eight minutes later, and South American players, officials, and fans broke into their opponents' dressing room after the match and attacked them. More than forty years later Ellis said, "It was a disgrace. In today's climate so many players would have been sent off the game would have been abandoned." Hungary (literally) fought their way to a 4–2 win.

They faced champions Uruguay in the semifinal, the unstoppable force against the immovable object: Hungary were unbeaten in four years, Uruguay had never lost a game in the tournament.

This time it was a thrilling sporting battle and Hungary won, 4–2, scoring twice in extra time, setting up a final date with West Germany, who had stormed past Austria, 6–1. The final, The Miracle of Bern, saw the Germans win, 3–2. They had lost to them, 8–3, two weeks earlier.

This World Cup is often overlooked, sandwiched between the drama of Brazil's stunning loss in 1950 and their swashbuckling Samba success of 1958. But it still holds the records for the highest average of goals per game (5.4) and the most goals scored by a team (Hungary, 27).

West Germany became the first country to win the tournament after losing a game, and it's the only time a nation has won it without playing a country from outside its own continent. They would have another important foe when they defended their title four years later.

## 1958 Sweden

Of the twenty World Cups up to 2014, Brazil had been to them all while Italy had only failed to qualify once. You know who kept them out of the 1958 finals? Little Northern Ireland, that's who.

After six tournaments the event matured from awkward adolescent to full-fledged adult. This version had four groups of four with the top two in each going through to the quarterfinal knockout stage. The structure would not change until 1974.

FIFA by now had divided qualification into continental zones, allocating a specific number of slots to each part of the world. Also, they instigated a rule that (other than the defending champions and hosts), countries could no longer qualify via withdrawals and that every finalist was required to play at least once.

In Europe, Italy only needed a tie in Northern Ireland to make it to Sweden while the home team required an unlikely victory. But the Hungarian referee got fog-bound in London and was unable to make the match. The Italians (understandably) refused to let an Irish referee take charge, so the game was played as an exhibition. It is known as The Battle of Belfast for the Italians' hard tackling, the crowd invading the field afterwards looking to exact revenge, and the visitors having to be escorted off by the home players. Ironically, the 2–2 result would have been good enough for Italy to qualify. Instead they returned six weeks later, the official (the manager of the Budapest Opera House, by the way) made it to Belfast on time, and the Irish won, 2–1. Once they made it to the finals, the Irish Football Association spent months arguing about whether to go (a majority of their members were against playing on Sundays).

Joining Northern Ireland were all three other British countries: England, Scotland, and Wales, though the Welsh were fortunate to make what remains their solitary appearance. Both Israel and Turkey had been placed in the Asian/African region and Turkey withdrew in protest because of the Arab-Israeli conflict, so Israel advanced to play Indonesia, who also pulled out for the same reason and Israel were then paired with Sudan, who declined the invitation as well. After three rounds of walkovers Israel were in the World Cup. However FIFA's new law that every finalist must play at least once led them to a random draw of countries which had finished runners-up in qualifying, "lucky losers" if you will. Uruguay refused the offer, as did Belgium, next out were Wales who jumped at the chance. They dispatched the Israelis and made it to the finals—technically representing Africa and Asia.

In Sweden, Scotland carried on from where they left off in 1954 and didn't win a game, England also went out in the first round, their 0–0 result with Brazil the first scoreless tie in World Cup history. A seventeen-year-old Pelé debuted for the South Americans in their final group game alongside the sparkling right-winger Garrincha. For the next eight years, Brazil never lost if those two started in the team, winning thirty-six out of forty matches.

Northern Ireland made the last eight despite winding up in the toughest group with West Germany, Czechoslovakia, and Argentina, who were back after an absence of twenty-eight years. The Irish shocked the Czechs in a 1–0 win then lost, 3–1, to the South Americans. When Czechoslovakia destroyed the Argentinians, 6–1, it left the Irish needing a tie against the world champions to force a playoff. Extraordinarily, they twice led the Germans but were pegged back both times, the contest finishing 2–2. They then beat the Czechs again, 2–1, in the playoff.

However, the quarterfinal against France, their fourth match in only eight days, was a bridge too far for the Irish walking wounded. Both goalkeepers were injured and to save money they had arrived with just seventeen players rather than the twenty-two allowed, an example of the rank amateurism infecting the whole campaign that had the battered and bruised squad travel more than 200 miles by bus the day before the game. Manchester United keeper and Munich air disaster hero Harry Gregg was voted the Goalkeeper of the Tournament.

In one semifinal, Pelé scored a hat trick in the space of 23 minutes as Brazil steamrollered the French, 5–2; hosts Sweden beat the champions West Germany, 3–1, in the other to set up the first final with countries from different continents.

In the only European World Cup not won by a European country, the South Americans were 2–1 ahead when Pelé scored twice,
his memorable first an outrageous, impudent chip over the defender
before burying it on the volley into the net. Brazil ran out 5–2 winners. Pelé is the youngest player to have scored in the championship
game, Swede Nils Liedholm at almost thirty-six the oldest.

It had taken eight years, but the ghost of the Maracanazo was
laid to rest.

## 1962 Chile

Remember when I wrote that FIFA had the qualification process
sorted? Yeah, I lied.

It was the decade man made it to the moon: the mind boggles
at how much of a struggle it was for the greatest minds in the
soccer universe to hone fifty-odd countries down to fourteen for a
quadrennial competition.

Perversely, FIFA wanted to expand the World Cup by limit-
ing it to Europe and South America. The winners of the North
American, African, and Asian zones were not guaranteed spots
but had to play off against countries from the two strongest continents. It led to a bewildering array of intercontinental series leading to the conclusion that FIFA's planning and execution were as
obtuse, opaque, and confusing as possible.

The European sections, for instance, had some with two
teams, some with three, and one with five. One even contained
Ethiopia! In Africa, Sudan and the United Arab Republic were
paired together, but *both* withdrew because FIFA refused to let
them play outside of the monsoon season, leaving the final round
one team short.

For this World Cup, goal average was used to separate teams tied on points in the first round; a country's total goals scored would be divided by the total they conceded, and whichever nation's average was higher would advance (Argentina is the only country ever eliminated by this method). This was the tournament the average number of goals per game fell below three, where it has since stayed. Just eight years previously, remember, it had been 5.4.

In 1960 the hosts suffered the Valdivia earthquake, the largest ever recorded, and it wrecked all but four stadiums earmarked for the tournament. The country's remoteness, devastated infrastructure, and lack of visiting fans created a low-key and poorly attended competition.

The Brazil vs. England quarterfinal was won by Garrincha, the "little bird," who tormented the English defense with a goal and an assist as they ran out 3–1 winners. During the match a stray dog wandered onto the field—again, endemic of the half-baked organization—and evaded all attempts at capture. Eventually striker Jimmy Greaves grabbed it, but as he carried it off it urinated down his white shirt. The mongrel was raffled off to the Brazilian squad and won, fittingly enough, by Garrincha.

Czechoslovakia beat Yugoslavia, 3–1, in Vina del Mar in front of fewer than 6,000 spectators in one semifinal, in contrast almost 80,000 packed into a sold-out stadium in Santiago to see the hosts lose, 4–2, to Brazil. Both Garrincha and Chile's Honorino Landa were sent off, and as the Brazilian trudged back to the locker room his head was split open by a bottle thrown from the crowd. But he was pardoned and allowed to play in the final.

In the championship match Brazil, even without Pelé who had been missing since tearing a leg muscle in the second game, were too good for the Eastern Europeans and won, 3–1. They joined Italy as the second nation to successfully defend their title.

## 1966 England

If ever a World Cup win defined an era, it was England's victory as host nation. The Swinging Sixties, a period when London was the epicenter of the world, a city bursting with artistic creativity as bands like the Beatles and the Stones conquered America and fashion icons and models strutted down Carnaby Street to end decades of a drab, dull, and dreary postwar funk. This was the first tournament widely filmed in color, even England not wearing their white uniform in the final seemingly preordained as an explosion of vibrant red streaked across newsreels and movie houses around the UK and beyond.

But before that, there were withdrawals and boycotts in qualifying. FIFA allocated a solitary slot to be shared among Africa, Asia, and Oceania, and most of the African countries pulled out in protest. South Africa, the one country who did want to take part, was banned because they practiced the racial policy of apartheid. North Korea eventually emerged from the compromised and complicated three-continental system. In Europe (containing Syria this time for some reason), a George Best-inspired Northern Ireland came within 13 minutes of forcing Switzerland into a playoff for a finals' place: needing to win in Albania, they were leading, 1–0, up until a late equalizer.

This tournament saw an upsurge in heavy tackles bordering on thuggery; dangerous skilled players were targeted by the opposition determined to stop them dribbling. The World Cup was still neither the marketing marvel nor the sporting spectacle it would become; the France vs. Uruguay contest was moved away from Wembley because the owners refused to cancel the regular Friday evening weekly greyhound racing!

In the first round, double-defending champions Brazil went out as they lost in the World Cup for the first time in twelve years, beaten 3–1 by Hungary while an even bigger shock was Italy's 1–0 loss to North Korea. In the quarterfinal, the Koreans rushed to a 3–0 lead after 25 minutes against Portugal, but four goals from Eusebio helped them to a 5–3 victory. The elfin elusive enigmatic Koreans captured the hearts of the British public then disappeared back into the isolationism of their curious Cold War-obsessed homeland. It would be forty-four years before they reappeared at the World Cup.

West Germany beat Uruguay, who had two men sent off in the space of five minutes by an English referee, 4–0. Meanwhile at Wembley, a West German official dismissed Argentina captain Antonio Rattin in their 1–0 quarterfinal loss to the hosts. He refused to leave the field and the police had to drag him away. Afterwards, England coach Alf Ramsey ran onto the field to physically prevent his players exchanging shirts with their opponents and called them "animals." The bad blood between the nations lingered and festered . . . the Argentinians still refer to the contest as *el robo del siglo* (the theft of the century).

England then beat Portugal, 2–1, and the Germans overcame the Soviet Union by the same score to lead us to one of the best, if not *the* best, final ever.

It remains the most-watched event in UK television history. England had conceded just one goal in the five previous games, but within 12 minutes Germany led, 1–0. Geoff Hurst leveled for the hosts and they then went ahead on a 78th minute goal by

Martin Peters. But with just seconds remaining, and the whole of England poised to celebrate like it was VE Day again, Wolfgang Weber prodded home to force extra time.

England's third goal is the most discussed and dissected in World Cup history. Hurst struck a fierce shot against the bar that ricocheted straight down, bounced once, and was cleared. Technical studies, forensic analysis of the footage, and examination of still shots have since proved the whole of the ball never crossed the line.

The Swiss referee consulted the Azerbaijani linesman and a few nods and gestures later, England were ahead. In the dying

Was it in? English number 10, Geoff Hurst, appeals for the goal while the German players claim the ball never crossed the line in extra time of the 1966 final at Wembley.

seconds, as the Germans attacked like a drug-fueled Panzer division in search of the equalizer that would have forced a replay, Hurst broke away and slammed home another. Fans had already invaded the field in celebration and it's the only final goal scored with spectators on the grass. Hurst is the only player to notch a hat trick in the championship match.

The Queen handed over the trophy and England became the first hosts in thirty-two years to be crowned champions. "Two world wars and one world cup," sing the English fans even today. But the Germans did not have to wait long to get their revenge.

## 1970 Mexico

There was color newsreel footage of the 1966 World Cup, but this edition was the first to be beamed around the planet in gorgeous, glorious, full-saturation technicolor. To soccer fans of a certain generation it's the definitive tournament: the vivid yellow shirts and bright blue shorts of Brazil; the blistering heat haze shimmering through the screen from noon kickoffs in the sweltering Mexican summer; memorable moments with the greatest stars the sport has seen. Franz Beckenbauer rallying the Germans in the quarterfinal, England goalkeeper Gordon Banks leaping across the goal to make one of the greatest saves ever filmed against Brazil, Pelé cementing his place as a legend in his final bow on the world stage with a supporting cast stuffed with an embarrassment of riches including Alberto, Jairzinho, Rivelino, and Tostão. They won every qualifying game and every match at the finals. Many consider this incarnation of the seleção the greatest team in history.

This World Cup sparked a full-blown conflict in Central America. The "Football War" between El Salvador and Honduras left 3,000 soldiers and civilians dead and displaced more than a quarter of a million people. Tensions between the neighbors were exacerbated by new Honduran laws aimed at Salvadoran immigrants, and when El Salvador won a qualification playoff in neutral Mexico City, they followed it up with an invasion. It wasn't until the 1980s that they finally signed a peace treaty.

Israel qualified from the most diverse, furthest-flung, wide-ranging qualification section ever: Israel, New Zealand, Rhodesia, Australia, Japan, and South Korea. Meanwhile, after the mass pullout debacle of the previous tournament, FIFA gave Africa an automatic place at the finals. Of course, Morocco then threatened to withdraw unless they were kept apart from the Israelis.

The first tournament staged outside South America and Europe saw the introduction of tactical substitutes, and goal difference (the figure you were left with when you subtracted the goals you conceded from the goals you scored) was the new tiebreaker. What happened if two teams had the same goal difference does not seem to have occurred to anyone: the Mexicans and Soviets ended level on points and goal difference and the group winner was decided by drawing lots anyway.

The England vs. West Germany quarterfinal was a rematch of the 1966 final and another exhilarating roller-coaster. The English led, 2–0, with just 22 minutes to play. Despite Beckenbauer pulling one back, Ramsey substituted two veteran midfielders to preserve them for the semifinal and the Germans equalized. The comeback was complete when they won it in extra time, their first-ever competitive victory over England. Some commentators blame the British government's surprise general election defeat four days later on the result. In the semifinal dubbed The Game of the Century, the Germans again went to extra time, but the Italians triumphed, 4–3, to meet Brazil who had seen off Uruguay, 3–1.

Both finalists had lifted the trophy twice so whoever won it would keep it permanently. Pelé opened the scoring but Italy equalized, then two goals in five second-half minutes from Gerson and Jairzinho (setting a record as the only man to score in every finals match) made it 3–1. Their fourth goal is one of the most famous in World Cup history, a few seconds of action crystallizing the dazzling display.

The move starts deep in the left back position, the Brazilians toying and teasing the Italians who know the jig is up. They take

Superstar Pelé is hoisted aloft after Brazil's era-defining 4–1 win over Italy in the 1970 final at Mexico City's famous Azteca stadium.

it in turns to run rings around their exhausted opponents or dribble past them before the ball ends up with Pelé on the edge of the Italian penalty box—the eighth Brazilian involved in the play. It looks like he rolls the ball sideways into an empty space, but what you don't see because it is out of camera shot is that captain Carlos Alberto is arriving like an express train. He cracks the ball so hard it looks like he is preparing for takeoff and it flies into the net.

Mário Zagallo, part of both the 1958 and 1962 squads, became the first man to win the tournament as both a player and coach. Brazil had won three out of the previous four World Cups. It would be a generation before they managed it again.

## 1974 West Germany

Two decades after the Miracle of Bern, West Germany did it again. They were crowned champions after overcoming a fancied European nation who were blessed with a golden generation of an embarrassment of riches. As had happened to Brazil in 1950, the defeat damaged not just the Dutch players, but the psychology of the whole country. The Dutch, the memories of the Nazi occupation still raw, expected revenge and redemption; instead they found dismay and disbelief. They call it, "The lost final."

The usual qualification controversy arrived with the Soviet Union pulling out in protest at human rights' violations. Kettle, pot, black, anyone? The final finals spot would be decided by a two-legged series between the Soviets and Chile and the first match ended scoreless in Moscow. In Chile, the democratically-elected government had been overthrown and the national stadium in Santiago changed into a detention (and torture) center for 7,000 "undesirables."

FIFA's delegates inspected the venue and reported that everything was hunky-dory (the prisoners had been bused to a desert salt-mining town), but the Soviets refused to travel and Chile were awarded a walkover. FIFA insisted that the contest go ahead—even though there was only one team on the field—so Chile kicked off and walked the ball into the empty net.

And yet again they tinkered with the format. This time the two qualifiers from the four first-round groups made up a further two sections of four teams in a second round-robin stage, the winners of each meeting in the final. Scotland made history as the first team ever eliminated without losing a match and arrived home before their postcards once more.

The imperious Dutch were built around the all-conquering Ajax club who won three European Cups between 1971 and 1973 (Johann Cruyff, playing in a special shirt with two stripes because he was personally sponsored by Puma and not the team supplier Adidas, first unveiled the iconic "Cruyff Turn" against Sweden). Coaches talk about needing a strong "spine" in a team, clutch players you can rely on, but this lot had a backbone made out of titanium it was so talented. They majestically swept aside Brazil to secure a place in the final.

The Germans were waiting for them after defeating Poland ("Not for the first time," World War II buffs are thinking) so it pitted Beckenbauer against Cruyff, the two greatest players on the planet following Pelé's retirement.

In retrospect, scoring so quickly was the worst thing that could have happened to Holland. Within 63 seconds they led 1–0 before a German had even touched the ball, Johan Neeskens converting a penalty won by Cruyff. In later years the Dutch admitted they didn't just want to win the game, they wanted to humiliate their opponents in the first competitive meeting between the nations. Wim van Hanegem had lost his father, his two brothers and his sister, while nearly every player's parents had suffered in World War II.

There had never been a penalty awarded in the previous ten finals, but within the first 25 minutes this final had two and the Germans were level. Two minutes before the break they were 2–1 up and Cruyff was booked at halftime on the walk to the locker room for arguing with the official.

It was the Dutch to a tee: fluid, interchangeable players with unbelievable skills but whose fractious, self-destructive nature was never far away. They huffed and puffed in the second half but for the second time in twenty years, the overwhelming favorites in the biggest soccer showdown had blown it by underestimating the Germans.

## 1978 Argentina

The first World Cup I remember.

It was half-a-world away literally and a million miles away metaphorically, enticing and exciting to an eight-year-old in drizzly, mizzly Northern Ireland who was transported to stadiums with tens of thousands of newspaper-carrying spectators. They tore them to shreds and in a choreographed littering extravaganza released the paper into the air, the pieces fluttering around the arena and resting on the fields like confetti at a giant's wedding. It was all so foreign and mesmerizing.

Now I know it was a facade, a tournament held against the backdrop of a brutal, ruthless dictatorship, a military junta carrying out a secret "Dirty War" on its own people. While I was worried about slate-gray clouds over Belfast, gun-metal gray was what concerned the people of Buenos Aires (the Germans were visited at their training camp by war "hero" Hans-Ulrich Rudel, a committed and unrepentant Nazi who had been a military adviser to Juan Perón. He fled to Argentina in 1948 to set up a relief organization for Third Reich fugitives who had escaped to Latin America). Journalists moaned that if it had been staged in any other country, Argentina would not have won it: like those medieval theologian scholars who would sit for hours discussing how many angels could fit on the head of a pin, it was a pointless waste of time. Win it they did.

The eleventh World Cup was the last with sixteen teams (even if sixteen didn't always turn up), and so it was the hardest to qualify for with 107 countries vying for fourteen slots. But if you tuned in late to watch France vs. Hungary you might have wondered who was playing. Both sides had only arrived with white change shirts, so officials tracked down the uniform of the local team and Les Blues played in green-and-white stripes. This was the third time in the World Cup a country had to borrow shirts—in a way it was comforting how amateurish it remained.

The first-round drama and entertainment was provided by a laughably euphoric and overconfident Scotland, who recorded a song claiming they would, "Win the World Cup." Their scouting was nonexistent and they lost, 3–1, to Peru thanks to a brace (two goals) from their danger man Teófilo Cubillas, whom they left criminally unattended; he had been voted the best young player at the 1970 World Cup and was South American Footballer of the Year in 1972.

Winger Willie Johnston was expelled after failing a drug test and Glaswegians bought copies of their World Cup record, now selling for a penny, to smash them in the street. Against Iran they were gift-wrapped the lead after one of the most hilarious own goals of all time, but the Iranians deservedly leveled; their rally to beat the Dutch was in vain.

Holland was missing Cruyff, who had refused to travel to Argentina. It was reported it was a protest against the human rights abuses of the military dictatorship, but thirty years later he said there had been a kidnap attempt on his family in 1977 and he was not prepared to leave them alone in Barcelona for weeks. Even without him they beat Italy, 2–1, to make it to their second final in a row.

In the last round of matches in the other group, Brazil beat Poland, 3–1, while Argentina's game against Peru kicked off an hour later. The hosts, who needed victory by a margin of four goals to reach the final, cruised home, 6–0.

Rumors swirled that the result was fixed, that the Argentinians threatened to withhold grain shipments, that the release of political prisoners was used as a bargaining chip, even that the eccentric Peruvian goalkeeper Ramon Quiroga, with frequent dashes to the halfway line, was a secret agent (he had been born in Argentina). What's not disputed is that junta leader General Jorge Rafael Videla visited Peru's locker room beforehand and impressed upon them the concept of Latin American brotherhood.

Peru had conceded just six goals in the preceding five matches combined—they let in as many in the space of 51 minutes. A feckless and toothless FIFA repeated the scheduling mistake four years later. Brazil complained and went home unbeaten in six games.

I watched the final with my dad in our small bungalow in the Belfast suburb of Dundonald. I remember the ticker-tape flurrying around the stands, a swirling snowstorm of streamers, the delayed start, the Argentinians coming out late, making the Dutch wait, then complaining about the plaster cast on René van de Kerkhof's wrist. Gamesmanship. The British commentator was disgusted by the pernicious, pathetic tactics.

Mario Kempes put the hosts ahead before substitute Dick Nanninga equalized with a towering header. In injury time, tragically, Rob Rensenbrink hit the post from a tight angle and the ball bounced to safety. I often wonder if that close-range shot gave him nightmares. A few inches over and Holland would have been world champions. Instead it was extra time. Kempes scored his second with a carbon copy of his first and Daniel Bertoni made it 3–1. The Dutch were the bridesmaids for the second successive World Cup. After back-to-back finals they wouldn't even qualify for the expanded edition four years later.

## 1982 Spain

My World Cup.

An excited twelve-year-old, two weeks in the heat of southern Spain entrancing me like dawn on Christmas Day. I was at the three first-round matches Northern Ireland played, culminating in the most longshot of wins over the hosts.

After fifty-two years, FIFA increased the participants from sixteen to twenty-four and for the first time more than 100 countries played a qualifier. Lesser-known soccer nations such as Kuwait and New Zealand took their bow, and you couldn't deny the Kiwis didn't deserve their place as they had slogged through an incredible 55,000 miles of travel. For the first time, countries from all six continental regions made the tournament.

Both England and Scotland qualified along with the Irish but all three British nations considered pulling out in reponse to the Falklands War. The Argentinian military junta had invaded the British islands off their coast two months prior to the World Cup and the UK sent a task force to the South Atlantic. With the countries at war and potentially having to meet on the soccer field, a withdrawal was discussed, but the South Americans surrendered the day after the finals began.

Yet another format reorganization saw the twenty-four teams divided into six groups of four with the top two advancing to the second stage. The draw itself was a farce. The names were in miniature soccer balls spun in drums but one of the bingo-style cages broke, while those doing the drawing forgot the regulations regarding who could play where and the sections had to be realigned. Spain's reputation for being disorganized and backward seemed well won.

This tournament was a slow burner that took a while to catch fire, but when it eventually sparked to life, it produced two of the greatest games in history.

It started with a shock, holders Argentina beaten by Belgium. In the same group, Hungary ran up a record-breaking 10 goals against the hapless El Salvadorians. Speaking of hapless, Scotland was on a mission to find even more hilarious ways to shoot themselves in the foot. They went out for the third successive tournament on goal difference, two of their defenders tackling each other to allow the USSR to score.

And so to Group Five, containing Northern Ireland, Spain, Yugoslavia, and Honduras in the cities of Zaragoza and Valencia. Northern Ireland's first match was against Yugoslavia, and on the morning of the game, two fans that had been to see Spain and

Honduras tie, 1–1, the previous evening said, "Northern Ireland will qualify from this group, no bother." This may be the only optimistic statement I've ever heard any Northern Irish soccer fan say.

We played well that night, Norman Whiteside at just seventeen years and forty-one days beating Pelé's record as the youngest-ever player in the finals, and it finished goalless. But we followed it up with a disappointing 1–1 tie against Honduras, leaving us needing to beat Spain in the final game to get through to the next round. We won, 1–0, despite having a man sent off, and I got to witness the most fantastic result in the history of the Irish Football Association.

The dozen countries left were separated into three groups of four, the group winners advancing to the semifinals. In the standout contest, Italy needed to beat Brazil to make the last four. I remember walking into my living room straight from school and being captivated by this match as only a child can. Italy opened the scoring through Paolo Rossi, a striker who had been recalled to the national team after serving a two-year ban in a betting scandal. The South Americans leveled, Rossi scored his second, and it took Brazil until the 68th minute to achieve parity once more. But rather than shut up shop they continued to attack and left gaps at the back, and with a quarter of an hour to go, Rossi sealed an unlikely hat trick and Brazil were out. The 1982 Brazil squad joined Hungary in 1954 and Holland in 1974 as the greatest teams to never win the tournament. In Brazil the match is called "The Disaster of Sarria."

We had returned home after our Spanish sojourn and like the rest of the country, I was glued to the TV as we took on Austria. We went 1–0 up through beanpole striker Billy Hamilton then the Austrians struck back twice to take the lead, but with 15 minutes to go up popped Hamilton again with the slowest header of all time to equalize. Years later he lived in the same small town I settled in outside Belfast and we would often go to the same trivia night at the local bar. One night I beat him in a head-to-head playoff but gave him my prize to thank him for those goals.

It set up a Sunday showdown with France for the semifinal— one of our part-time players declined to be named on the bench because it was the Sabbath. It is surreal that we were 90 minutes away from a World Cup semifinal. And we should have taken the lead, captain Martin O'Neill's strike horrendously ruled out for handball by the Polish referee when it was nowhere near his hand. Could we have held out and mounted an Alamo-style defense like we had against the Spaniards?

Who knows? Instead, as had happened in Sweden twenty-four years earlier, the Irish simply ran out of steam and France won, 4–1. It had been a wonderful, whimsical campaign and my mum took me into terrorist-torn Belfast as thousands of fans lined the streets to welcome the squad home. France lost the semifinal on penalties to West Germany while Italy defeated Poland.

Every non-German was rooting for Italy after the Disgrace of Gijon (see Chapter Four) and because paradoxically it was the Italians who had exploded into life, while the Germans who (the semifinal aside) had been craven and uninspiring.

The Italians missed a penalty but Rossi's header put them in front, then Marco Tardelli doubled the lead with an iconic goal, remembered not for the execution (a fine low strike from the edge of the box) but for the celebration. Anyone who watched it can still recall it: Tardelli running while pumping his arms, his face a mixture of disbelief and utter joy as he screams, the camera shot capturing it head-on as his teammates struggle to catch and congratulate him. The moment is cemented in Italian culture as "Tardelli's Scream."

Italy won, 3–1, and joined Brazil with three World Cup wins. At forty, goalkeeper Dino Zoff became the oldest man ever to lift the trophy.

## 1986 Mexico

The 1986 World Cup belied the old adage that one man doesn't make a team. When that man is Diego Maradona, it does.

He won the tournament for Argentina. I don't mean he was the MVP of the final, I mean that if it wasn't for him they would not have been champions. His skill, his determination, his trickery, his ability to bamboozle opponents and leave them with spinning, twisted heads like Regan in *The Exorcist* . . . the stocky, mercurial midfield wizard scored five and assisted on another five, one strike regularly voted the best goal of all time.

Before that though, the Germans lost a World Cup qualifier for the first time in history after thirty-six matches (Portugal the victor), and Iraq were competition debutantes despite playing all their home games in neutral venues because of the Iran/Iraq War.

Mexico became the first country to host the World Cup twice with just three tournaments separating both versions (Colombia, who had been awarded it in 1974, pulled out because they could not afford it). Once more, FIFA messed with the format. It started with six groups of four, but rather than a second group stage it went straight to a last-16 knockout round, so the top two in each group made the next round along with four third-place countries.

For the second successive World Cup, England, Scotland, and Northern Ireland all qualified. I was a hormone-ridden sixteen-year-old in the middle of important exams, but my dad was still willing to take me. It was the most illustrious period of Irish soccer history when our wee country was bestriding the world like a colossus. In the space of four years we won the British Championship twice, before that we had only won it once since 1884! We qualified for back-to-back World Cups and were just a few minutes away from making the 1984 European Championships at the expense of mighty West Germany after beating them home and away in qualifying. If I had known back then that more than three decades later we still have not qualified again, I would have jumped at the chance and repeated my exams the following year. I'd probably still be at school now. But I declined and spent the World Cup revising and writing essays about the 19th century unification of Italy and the use of metaphor in Tess of the D'Urbervilles.

Scotland went into the final group game against Uruguay needing a win to advance, and inside 60 seconds their job got a lot easier as Jose Batista entered the record books as the fastest dismissal in World Cup history (he said when he returned to the dressing room, the equipment man asked, "How can you get sent off when they're still playing the national anthem?"). But they couldn't find a way through; afterwards Scottish officials labeled their opponents a "disgrace" and "scum."

Northern Ireland joined our Celtic cousins on the plane home. Against Algeria, they took the lead after just six minutes but the Africans equalized. We then lost unluckily, 2–1, to Spain, and went out with a 3–0 defeat to Brazil in goalkeeper Pat Jennings's final game on his forty-first birthday.

The last 16 contest between the Soviet Union and Belgium was one of the most exciting games I have ever watched. It was 2–2 at full-time, the Belgians scored twice, the Soviets clawed one back within a minute and the action oscillated between both goalmouths like a spectator's head at a high-paced tennis match. Igor Belanov, European Player of the Year in 1986, became the third player in World Cup history to score a hat trick but finish on the losing side.

In the semifinal, a repeat of the 1982 clash, the Germans again overcame the French. In the other last-four contest between Argentina and Belgium, Maradona executed exactly the same thing he had done three days previously against England (his wonder goal, not the Hand of God). He opened the scoring, then another superlative solo effort that had him pivoting and pirouetting past four bemused Belgians made the game safe.

So, South America against Europe at the Azteca stadium again in front of a record final attendance of almost 115,000— 7,000 more than the 1970 final. Franz Beckenbauer, now in charge of West Germany under the title "team supervisor" because he lacked the necessary qualifications, sacrificed midfield creativity and ordered Lothar Matthäus to man-mark Maradona. The Argentinians were two goals to the good with a quarter of an hour left but Karl-Heinz Rummenigge pulled one back, Beckenbauer gambled and freed up Matthäus, substitute Rudi Völler leveled it up.

Maradona to the rescue. With six minutes left his exquisite, perfectly-weighted pass released Jorge Burruchaga, whose clinical finish made it 3–2. Beckenbauer became the first man to lose the final both as a player and a coach, but more pertinently Maradona became the first man to win the tournament single-handedly.

## 1990 Italy

The 1990 World Cup was a low-scoring, negative tournament that often appeared to be a war of attrition rather than the biggest sporting event on earth.

I was living in England, a country that remembers that summer fondly. The BBC's theme music for their coverage, Puccini's operatic "Nessun Dorma," even now is synonymous with soccer success, and more than a quarter of a century later, Leicester City used it to celebrate their fairy-tale Premier League title. It is the only time England managed to reach the semifinals outside of their own country.

It was a sterile affair with a record-low average of 2.2 goals per game and the first team to fail to score in the championship match. It featured a record number of 16 red cards, including the first in the final—two dismissals, in fact. Play was so negative and cautious that it led to two rule changes: passing the ball back to the goalkeeper was outlawed, and a win would be worth three points instead of two in an effort to reward attacking play.

Mexico had been expelled for fielding overage players in the 1988 Olympics, but it wasn't the only skullduggery in the Americas. Chile was losing to Brazil at the Maracanã when goalkeeper Roberto Rojas collapsed, having seemingly been hit by a flare thrown from the crowd. With blood streaming from his head wound, he was helped off the field and the match abandoned. It appeared Chile would be awarded the points and that Brazil would miss out on the finals for the first time ever.

However, the next day photographs emerged showing that the flare had landed a yard away, and Rojas—who played in Brazil for Sao Paulo!—had used a razor blade hidden in his gloves to cut his head. Chile were kicked out of the next World Cup and Rojas, the team doctor, and the coach all received bans. Remarkably, the Brazilians apparently forgave Rojas as he later coached Sao Paulo.

Cameroon became the first African nation to reach the quarter-finals, while West Germany and Holland renewed their rivalry in Milan's famed San Siro stadium, home to both Inter and AC. Adding spice was that Germany had three Inter stars, Andreas Brehme, Lothar Matthäus, and Jürgen Klinsmann; the Dutch boasted the famed trio from AC, Marco van Basten, Ruud Gullit, and Frank Rijkaard. Both sides were down to ten men when Rudi Völler and Rijkaard were red-carded, TV cameras caught Rijkaard spitting on Völler as they left the field, and the Germans ran out 2–1 winners.

In the semifinals, it was Argentina vs. Italy and England vs. West Germany, four World Cup winners. Both semifinals finished 1–1 before going to penalties as the lack of anything creative or new continued. The South Americans won their shootout in Naples, as did the Germans in Turin, to set up the only final to be a repeat of the previous tournament. Europeans would defeat South Americans for the first time in a championship match.

The Argentinians received 22 yellow cards in Italy and had four players suspended. They wanted to hold out for penalties and managed just one shot on target the whole game. Pedro Monzón became the first player sent off in the final for a dangerous challenge on future USA coach Klinsmann and Gustavo Dezotti was also ejected with three minutes to go.

Still, the Germans left it late, winning with a penalty, fittingly in the circumstances, five minutes from time. They had avenged

1986 and Beckenbauer was the second man to win the competition as player and coach, the last hurrah for West Germany before German reunification.

It was a cynical, sour, unpleasant finish to an ugly tournament. But there was a bright dawn ahead—the next World Cup crossed the ocean and entered a Brave New World.

# 1994 USA

This was going to be the year the soccer sky fell, the sporting world collapsed, and life would never be the same again because those brash, know-nothing Yanks would ruin football. Hell, they don't even call it "football."

That was the view of many crotchety European pundits and journalists as the tournament was staged in the USA. It would undoubtedly be a disaster as FIFA had sold the sport's soul to reap the sponsorship rewards thrust at them by soda companies and candy bar manufacturers. The experts were convinced the Americans would glamorize, glorify, and ruin the beautiful game.

This wasn't sour grapes at all—for the only time in history none of the four British home nations had made the finals, and the USA had even beaten England in the 1993 US Cup leading to the headline in my old newspaper, *The Sun*, of "Yanks 2, Planks 0." TV presenters in the UK mocked the terminology used stateside: "offense" instead of "attack," "set plays" instead of "set pieces," and worst of all, "PKs" instead of "penalties." The Americans incited the traditionalists by holding the draw in glitzy brash Las Vegas: instead of a slew of retired, venerated, and dignified players onstage, those crazy, showbiz-obsessed Yanks recruited comedian Robin Williams, actor Beau Bridges, and model Carol Alt.

In the event, the naysayers were proved wrong, the doubting Thomases converted, the Old World eclipsed by the New. In return for receiving the World Cup, the USA had committed to creating a professional league, and now Major League Soccer's average attendance is the seventh largest in the world, ahead of Argentina, Brazil, France, and Holland. The average crowd of nearly 69,000 per match has never been bettered, the total attendance of more than 3.5 million fans still a record even though the competition has since expanded, spectacular figures for a country whose national sport is a different kind of football.

Brazil were the favorites despite their first qualification defeat ever, their 31-match unbeaten streak coming to an end in the altitude of Bolivia's La Paz. Cameroon's heroics in Italy led to an increase in Africa's representation from two to three and they carved the extra spot out of the CONCACAF and Oceania zones, forcing not one, but two, intercontinental playoffs. So after Australia beat Canada they had to navigate a home-and-away series against Argentina. A panicked nation recalled Maradona to the side even though he was patently unfit and overweight after a year's ban for testing positive for cocaine. They sneaked in thanks to an own goal, and by the time of the tournament he was leaner and fitter, his physical transformation both astounding and illegal.

He scored against Greece but failed a drug test for the banned stimulant ephedrine and was sent home, his glittering international career finished. Cameroon versus Russia in the group stage produced two records, Oleg Salenko scoring five times in a game, dancing Roger Milla the oldest scorer ever at forty-two.

Saudi Arabia was the surprise package, narrowly losing to the Dutch and then defeating both Morocco and Belgium. Look up Saeed Al-Owairan's stunning individual match-winner in the last match: picking the ball up deep in his own half he powers past five Belgians on a 60-yard run before scoring. It was Maradonaesque.

Compared to the dirge of Italia 90, the knockout stages were positively scintillating, Brazil the only non-Europeans left in the last eight. Roberto "The Divine Ponytail" Baggio scored twice to see Italy past Bulgaria in the semifinal. The Eastern Europeans— who had never even won a match in finals' history previously— had handed Germany their earliest knockout in thirty-two years in the quarterfinal. I went to the other semi at the Rose Bowl in Pasadena between Sweden and Brazil, Romario finally unlocking the Swedish defense with 10 minutes to go.

Unfortunately, for a country hooked on razzmatazz and show-manship, the final was a real letdown. It lacked the unpleasant histrionics of the 1990 showpiece, but both Italy and Brazil were terrified of losing, frightened of making a mistake, too timid to attack, too worried to take a chance.

The first final in which neither team scored was settled on penalties, and to prove the soccer gods had a wicked sense of humor, Italy's standout performer Baggio skied the crucial kick giving Brazil their fourth title. The tournament that had kicked off with Diana Ross missing a penalty in the opening ceremony finished with Baggio missing his. He looked on ruefully as another man who came equally close to glory, Vice President Al Gore, pre-sented the trophy to Brazilian captain Dunga.

# 1998 France

It took fifty-two years for the World Cup to be enlarged from six-teen teams, but with thirty-two countries in 1998 it had doubled in size within two decades. After sixty years it returned to France and ended with a triumphant host nation celebrating on a scale the country had not seen since liberation from the Germans.

Now with a straightforward eight groups of four, the top two in each section made the knockout rounds. The reorganization didn't stop Scotland from setting a new record—for the eighth time at the finals they failed to get out of their group.

In the last 16 their fellow Brits the English once more locked horns with their old rivals Argentina in the match of the tournament. A breathless opening saw a penalty awarded to each team within the first 10 minutes! England then went ahead through nineteen-year-old Michael Owen, his sensational individual effort considered one of his country's greatest goals, but on the stroke of halftime the South Americans tied it up with Javier Zanetti's cleverly-worked free kick.

Just two minutes into the second half, David Beckham was fouled by Argentina captain Diego Simeone. Beckham, lying on the ground, swung his leg at his opponent and Simeone collapsed like he had been downed by an Exocet missile. Beckham was sent off and Argentina won on penalties. Beckham was blamed for the loss by both the English press and the public (his effigy was burned in the streets) and he fled to join his Spice Girl wife on tour in America. A London tabloid ran with the headline, "10 Heroic Lions, One Stupid Boy." In the most ironic of ironies, Adidas had picked the day of the match to launch an ad referencing Maradona's Hand of God. It pictured Beckham with the slogan, "After tonight, England v Argentina will be remembered for what a player did with his feet."

In the last eight, the Argentineans met the Dutch, who gained revenge for their 1978 final defeat, Dennis Bergkamp winning it with seconds left when he expertly killed a high pass stone dead, cut inside, and unleashed a sublime shot into the net.

Croatia, France, and Brazil joined them in the last four. Both semifinals were gripping and decided by a narrow margin. Brazil put out the Dutch on penalties, France beat Croatia, 2–1, despite playing the last 15 minutes with 10 men. The hosts' goals came from right back Lilian Thuram—incredibly, in an international career spanning 15 years and 142 appearances, these were the only goals he ever scored! Two in the space of 23 minutes in a World Cup semifinal . . . talk about timing. For the first time since 1974, we had a new finalist.

France defeated Brazil, 3–0, and we also had the first new World Cup winner in 20 years. As the millennium dawned, the tournament was poised to expand its horizon and enter uncharted territory.

## 2002 Japan and South Korea

The new century opened with a double first as the World Cup went to Asia to be co-hosted by two countries. It is illustrative of how much the global soccer landscape had changed that there was barely a whisper about it going to a "non-football" destination compared to the furor that had greeted it being held in the USA just eight years previously.

Two different nations putting on the same competition was more an ethereal puzzle for the mind to accept than a literal logistical challenge: Japan's capital Tokyo and Seoul in South Korea are just 700 miles apart—in 1994 the USA team played in Detroit then four days later in Pasadena, a distance of 2,000 miles.

In the Land of the Rising Sun it was the rising soccer nations who umm, well, arose. More than any other tournament before or since this one belonged to the underdog with both South Korea and Turkey making the semifinals. But when it got down to the wire and the final two, we were left with our familiar friends, Germany and Brazil.

Germany had been forced into a playoff after a 5–1 humiliation at home to England, only their second qualification defeat in 63 matches. The British public voted it the second greatest sporting moment of all time—ahead of the 1966 final! England snatched the automatic spot in the third minute of injury time against Greece when a free kick was hammered home by . . . that stupid boy David Beckham. The villain who had been vilified by a nation was now the hero worshiped by a country (incidentally, Northern Ireland's form had deteriorated so dramatically that for this campaign we were fifth seeds alongside the likes of San Marino, Andorra, and Liechtenstein. I went to see us play Bulgaria in Sofia—even though we scored three goals we still lost, 4–3).

Meanwhile, the Oceania zone now had thirty-four countries but still lacked a dedicated berth, and it could be argued that quantity was at the expense of quality in the region as Australia beat Tonga, 22–0, American Samoa, 31–0 (a record), Fiji, 2–0, and Samoa, 11–0 in the space of a week.

From the opening day when Senegal stunned defending champions France it was clear that this was no ordinary tournament. The holders went out in the first round without scoring, Mexico sent home Croatia, who had been semifinalists in the previous competition, Japan eliminated Russia, the USA and South Korea saw off Poland and Portugal. Second favorites Argentina were also dumped out early by England, the pivotal contest broadcast at lunchtime in the UK, Beckham converting the crucial penalty. His redemption from sinner to saint was complete. Many stores did not reopen in England that afternoon as the public celebrated revenge for the Hand of God that had been sixteen years in the making.

As usual, England went out in the quarterfinals, this time to Brazil, Ronaldinho scoring with a 35-yard free kick that had stranded goalkeeper David Seaman flapping like an seal as the ball flew over his head. For the first time the last eight reflected a true global tournament with countries from Europe, North America, South America, Africa, and Asia all represented.

Germany beat South Korea in the last four but afterwards legend Franz Beckenbauer said, "Apart from [goalkeeper Oliver] Kahn, you could put that lot in a bag and beat it with a stick and whoever got hit would deserve it." It seemed harsh. Brazil eliminated Turkey in the other semifinal.

The countries had seven titles between them, but strangely this was their first World Cup meeting. It was Ronaldo's redemption. Beckham had gone from zero to hero but Ronaldo's metamorphosis was even more pronounced and potent. The zombie who shuffled around for 90 minutes in the final four years previously was replaced by the deadly marksman whose quick-fire double won the trophy.

They were the first champions to win all their games since they had done it themselves in 1970. It was their record fifth title. Captain Cafu appeared in a record third successive final. The Germans also went into the record books as they now had four defeats in the championship match but, in time, they too would settle the score against their conquerors.

## 2006 Germany

If the 2002 tournament was all about the underdog, then 2006 was regression to the mean. The success of the usual suspects felt like the World Cup returned to being the preserve of the big boys:

for a fleeting moment the kids got into the playroom and messed things up, but now the teenagers were home and ready to play pool, sneak beer, and wrestle back control.

One interloper who finally did make it to the finals was Australia. The poor Aussies, perennial confederation winners but losers in a series of increasingly heartbreaking intercontinental playoffs, booked their first World Cup date since 1974. They overcame two-time winners Uruguay in a heart-stopping penalty-kick showdown and for the first time in twenty-four years all six confederations were represented. The Socceroos were one of two outsiders (along with Ghana) to make the final sixteen—the other fourteen countries were a roll call of the same old, same old.

They tied Croatia despite English referee Graham Poll (why do so many refereeing controversies feature English officials?) neglecting to send off Josip Simunic after he received two yellow cards, and it was only when the Croat received a *third* yellow card three minutes later that he was ordered from the field.

Meanwhile, Russian official Valentin Ivanov probably needed a new set of cards after taking charge of The Battle of Nuremberg, the second-round clash between Portugal and Holland. He flourished a record sixteen yellow cards and four reds as each side finished with nine men.

Portugal's Costinha was dismissed before halftime, then the red card for Holland's Khalid Boulahrouz after an hour sparked a fight on the touchline with the Portuguese coaching staff. Another scuffle broke out when the Dutch did not return the ball after it was kicked out of play for an opponent to receive treatment. Deco became the second Portuguese sent off then, it was nine-a-side when Giovanni van Bronckhorst was given his marching orders as well. Somewhere in among the fighting, Portugal won, 1–0. In total, 345 yellow cards and 28 red cards were shown in this World Cup, an average of 5.4 yellows a match.

The last eight in 2002 included the USA, South Korea, Senegal, and Turkey. By contrast, these quarterfinalists featured six of the seven winners (Uruguay the odd team out). Switzerland became the first country to be knocked out without letting in a goal after being eliminated on penalty kicks.

Speaking of penalties . . . the young hosts were under the Teutonic tutelage of the charismatic Jürgen Klinsmann, repeatedly fending off criticism about him commuting from California. Their quarterfinal against Argentina went to spot kicks and goalkeeper Jens Lehmann took center stage with the most famous scrap of paper in German history.

Before each Argentinian kick, he paused and consulted a sheet of paper tucked in his sock that had been given to him by goalkeeping coach Andy Köpke. It contained notes on each penalty taker, but Lehmann later confessed he could not decipher the writing and only two of the seven players listed even took penalties! If it was a mind game designed to unsettle his opponents, it worked. The hosts won the shootout; the cheat sheet was auctioned for one million Euros for charity and is now on display in a museum of the Federal Republic of Germany in Bonn.

The Germans had never lost a competitive game in Dortmund, but in their semifinal the Italians scored in the last minute of extra time and again in injury time. They lined up against France, who had beaten Portugal thanks to a penalty scored by Zinedine Zidane. For the first time in twenty-eight years—and only the second occasion since 1938—neither Brazil nor Germany were in the final.

Italy won on penalty kicks after it finished 1–1 and so, to continue the theme of redemption, they won the World Cup on penalties after becoming the first nation to lose it by the same method in 1994. Another European nation went on a similar quest in the next final.

## 2010 South Africa

Apparently, FIFA was not just rotating through the continents but the narrative as well. In Germany the old warhorses dominated in the home of a traditional powerhouse, but it was the dark horses who excelled on the dark continent in 2010. A generation previous, Africa did not even have a representative at the World Cup; now South Africa edged out Morocco to hold it (more than a decade later it emerged in a New York federal court that American Chuck Blazer, a high-ranking FIFA executive, had accepted bribes in return for backing the South African bid and had turned FBI informant).

For the first time, more than 200 countries lined up to play, a startling explosion when you consider that just 20 years earlier there were 116 entrants. Australia had moved to Asia (so to speak) and qualified easily without having to criss cross the planet for a series of playoffs, while New Zealand also made it after beating Bahrain in one of those same intercontinental affairs. Australasia finally had two representatives, at least geographically, if not as defined by FIFA.

Markers led down in the qualifiers signposted what was to come. Spain became the first country to win all 10 matches, Holland with one country less in their section won all eight. These two would contest the final.

The holders, the runners-up, and the hosts all tumbled out in the first round. South Africa's fanatical voracious support couldn't stop the Rainbow Nation from becoming the first home country eliminated in the group stage. They still fared better than the French, who managed one goal and one point. Champions Italy also failed to advance, held to a tie by overperforming underdogs New Zealand, who went home with the consolation of being the only unbeaten team in the competition (three ties).

Only one out of six African countries (Ghana) qualified for the knockout round. It took eighty years for the tournament to get to the soccer-crazy continent; it was a shame that when it did, the actors who had starred in previous rehearsals fluffed their lines on opening night.

England faced Germany in the last 16 and it was the first occasion that extra time was not needed following their titanic battles in 1966, 1970, and 1990. If a Hollywood screenwriter had pitched what happened he would have been laughed out of the room. Forty-four years after Geoff Hurst's did it?/didn't it? shot was ruled a goal, a fierce strike by Frank Lampard hit the bar, bounced down, and clearly crossed the line. The Uruguayan official thought otherwise. Revenge may be a dish best served cold, but to wait almost half a century . . . It should have been 2–2 at halftime; instead Germany went on to win, 4–1, England's biggest-ever defeat at the finals. There is probably a German word for this kind of thing. Two years later, FIFA introduced goal-line technology.

The Dutch beat Brazil in the quarterfinal, the South Americans losing in normal time outside Europe for the first time in six decades. Holland then saw off Uruguay in the last four and for once their pacey, tricky individuals seemed to be harnessing and feeding off the team collective. Spain defeated Germany in the other semifinal thanks to a late thundering header by defender Carles Puyol, who only scored two other goals in his 13-year international career.

After 18 tournaments, for the first time ever, the championship match would not be contested by one of the big four: Brazil, Italy, Germany, or Argentina.

It was not third time lucky for Holland. I watched it with my Dutch friend Frank in New Orleans who was sure—absolutely 100 percent convinced—that after two previous failures, it was written in the stars that they would claim the title. It wasn't. They didn't.

Barcelona's Andrés Iniesta finally broke the deadlock with just four minutes of extra time remaining, a scratchy forgettable contest pockmarked with persistent fouling that ended with a record 14 cautions (nine Holland, five Spain) and John Heitinga of Holland red-carded. Spain became the eighth country to claim the trophy and the first Europeans to win it outside the continent. Their fans blew their vuvuzelas long into the night.

## 2014 Brazil

And so our journey down the World Cup road ends with the twentieth incarnation in 2014. It will forever be synonymous with one match: where did you watch Germany hammer Brazil, 7–1?

Previous decades saw a continual shifting in the balance of power between South America and Europe, but now the Europeans are in the ascendancy. The last three winners have been from Europe and they did it on three different continents. The last time a non-European country other than Brazil lifted the trophy was Argentina in 1986.

It's as if the World Cup story is on a loop of alternating plot lines. In 2002 the outsiders shone, in 2006 we went back to the traditional powerhouses, along came 2010 with more upsets, 2014 the upstarts put in their place. This was a tournament short on shocks—until the host's shocking humiliation in the semifinal and the most shocking shock of all time.

Goal-line technology was used for the first time to confirm France's goal against Honduras in the group stage, while Mexico versus Holland was stopped for the competition's first water break. Another innovation saw referees armed with vanishing foam to mark out 10 yards from a free kick in an effort to stop the wall encroaching.

All eight previous winners had qualified and three were drawn together: Italy, Uruguay, and England, along with Costa Rica. Italy beat England, 2–1 (hysterically, the England physiotherapist Gary Lewin was stretchered off with a dislocated ankle suffered celebrating England's equalizer!) and only needed a tie with Uruguay to advance.

Enter Luis Suárez, the villain of the South Americans' victory over Ghana last time out (see Chapter 6). He got involved in a bit of a scrap with defender Giorgio Chiellini; Uruguay won a corner from which they scored the winning goal. Replays showed that Suárez had bitten Chiellini, and Suárez, who had been banned in both Holland and England for biting, was suspended for nine international matches and all soccer related activity for four months. Once again, though, his "black arts" had worked—Uruguay went through.

Spain was knocked out after two matches, the fastest elimination of a defending champion since Italy in 1950. Their first game against Holland was a repeat of the 2010 final, but this time the Dutch ran rampant, their 5–1 victory the largest margin a holder had ever lost by. This hour-and-a-half seemed to have sounded the death knell for the Spaniards' glorious era of tiki-taka soccer.

Germany buried their 1982 embarrassment and beat Algeria to qualify for the quarterfinals for a staggering sixteenth successive time. They then put out France and became the first country to reach four straight semis.

The host's last-eight win over Colombia featured a record 54 fouls, and with two minutes left Juan Zuniga kneed Brazilian talisman Neymar in the back, causing a fractured vertebra and ending his tournament. Without the inspirational Neymar and suspended captain Thiago Silva, Brazil were given a shellacking by Germany in the last four. Another round, another record. It was the Germans' eighth final.

On the other side of the draw, Argentina and Holland, two nations with a rich World Cup history that included the 1978 final and the 1998 quarterfinal, conjured up the first scoreless semifinal ever. Argentina won on penalties to set up a repeat of the 1986 and 1990 finals against their old foe.

So sixty-four years after the Maracanazo, the final returned to the iconic Maracanã, and for the third successive tournament we needed extra time. German midfielder Sami Khedira withdrew after getting injured in the warm-up, then his understudy Christoph Kramer was taken off after half an hour suffering from concussion, but his replacement, André Schürrle, proved pivotal. It was his cross that was volleyed in by Mario Götze, and the scorer, who had only come on in the 88th minute, became the first substitute to notch a World Cup-winning goal.

Germany joined Italy as four-time winners (though it was their first title since reunification) and they became the first Europeans to win the World Cup in the Americas. In one final historical footnote, Götze's winner was the 171st goal of the tournament, equaling the record set in 1998.

That German juggernaut just keeps rolling.

Captain Philipp Lahm and his teammates celebrate Germany's fourth world title after defeating Argentina, 1–0, at the Maracanã Stadium, July 2014.

# CHAPTER TWO

# THE USA'S RUINOUS ROAD TO RUSSIA

Let's start with a forced, tangled metaphor. World Cup qualification should be plain sailing and not a pothole-strewn, obstacle-laden rocky road. It's an absolute disgrace that the USA will not be at the 2018 World Cup.

We are the third largest country on the planet by population with more than 300 million people. It shouldn't be difficult to field eleven players capable of ranking in the top three countries in North and Central America. That's not to dismiss the smaller nations—I'm from Northern Ireland and know the piranhas of international soccer can occasionally bring down a big fish—but it's the minimum we should expect.

Up until this cycle, the big bad bullies of the USA and Mexico had made the tournament a total of twenty-five times between them. All the other CONCACAF countries combined had mustered only fourteen appearances, and just three of those had managed it more than once.

We had been present at every tournament since 1990. To put that in perspective, of FIFA's 211 member countries only six others boast a similar record: Brazil and Argentina from South America, Germany, Italy, and Spain from Europe, and South Korea, who dominate Asia. That is serious big-hitting company to keep.

Admittedly international soccer has tightened up. Improvements in technological analysis and tactics, and the movement of experienced and talented coaches between countries, means traditionally weak soccer nations are no longer easy prey. These days, a well-drilled, well-marshaled, well-prepared, well-coached team can frustrate the big boys.

In 2000, en-route to my week-long bachelor party in New Orleans, we stopped off in Iceland to see Northern Ireland play a World Cup qualifier. Our 1–0 defeat was mourned as a disaster. But sixteen years later that same frozen island beat England to reach the quarterfinals of Euro 2016. The country with a population of around 320,000—smaller than sixty American cities and the size of Lexington, Kentucky—knocked out a World Cup winner made up of 53 million.

For the vast majority of nations international soccer is cyclical, and there will be periods when smaller places with a soccer heritage and tradition will produce talented players (e.g., Uruguay's population is just 3.4 million—less than Los Angeles—but they are double World Cup winners). However, since 1974, they have twice gone twelve years without even qualifying for the finals.

It's simple math: the more teenagers who play the sport, the more who continue to a higher level, the more who join professional clubs, the more who are exposed to high-level tactics and training—the better the national team. We are the biggest soccer-playing country on Earth in terms of population. There should be a conveyor belt of continuous talent.

At the 2014 World Cup we were officially ranked by FIFA as the 13th-best country in the world. What happened? How can a team on the cusp of being rated one of the top dozen soccer nations on the planet suddenly free fall so dramatically that they are not even good enough to make the next competition?

Let's examine the global qualification process. The World Cup is a showcase for the world game, and if it was only a competition for the very best nations then we could just pick the top four teams from Europe and South America and start with a final eight (all twenty tournaments have been won by countries from those continents, Europe leads 11–9). It's more than that.

The six confederations in FIFA choose their own format to fill their allocated berths. In Europe, UEFA (the Union of European Football Associations) seeded their members and created nine groups of six, each country playing home and away for a total of ten games. The section winners made it to Russia and four more countries qualified from playoffs featuring the best second-place teams. The strength in depth is such that France, Holland, and Sweden were all drawn together, while Spain and Italy—winners of two of the last three World Cups!—were in the same section so only one was guaranteed automatic qualification (by contrast Mexico made the 2014 finals despite only winning *three games* in the whole process against Panama, Jamaica, and a playoff victory over New Zealand!).

By comparison it's a cakewalk to qualify from the CONMEBOL region governing South America. Just ten nations play each other in a total of eighteen contests home and away. The top four make it to the finals while even the fifth has a second bite at it with an intercontinental playoff against the Oceania representative.

Africa has fifty-three countries, and the twenty nations remaining in the second round are put into five sections of four with all group champions making the finals. Similarly, the Asian region whittles its forty-six members down to twelve and creates two groups of six. After ten games the top two teams in each group go to the World Cup while the two countries finishing third have a playoff with the victor taking on the fourth-place finisher in the CONCACAF hexagonal, giving both another shot at making it (Australia versus Honduras this time).

The final region of the soccer world to (possibly) offer a path to the World Cup is the Oceania zone covering New Zealand and the other Pacific Islands. Australia left it in 2006 to join the Asian confederation in the expectation that with four guaranteed spots it provided a more accessible qualification route. (In April 2001 they annihilated American Samoa, 31–0, in a qualifier for the 2002 World Cup, the biggest victory in an international match ever. Archie Thompson broke the record for most goals scored in an international match with 13.)

There are only eleven members in this remote part of the world and they go through an involved and convoluted five rounds to finally find the two best teams. I assume it's a deliberate ploy to spin things out as long as possible to keep them occupied in the four years between tournaments. The champion takes on the fifth-best team in South America for a finals slot.

Here in CONCACAF (The Confederation of North, Central American and Caribbean Association Football), there are three rounds before the USA even enters. Months of elimination games featuring tiny Caribbean islands you would struggle to locate on a map such as Montserrat and Dominica to get to the point where the six top-rated teams join in.

While we can't be faulted for our geographical positioning, I think that not getting regularly tested against top-class opposition in competitive games, as opposed to meaningless exhibitions, is detrimental to the maturing and progression of the national team. I'm sure it's not a coincidence that every four years it's Europeans and South Americans who excel.

If it's so easy to make the finals, with qualifying no more than a minor irritant to the mighty American juggernaut, what went wrong this time?

The USA had done well at the 2014 tournament, escaping the Group of Death with eventual winners Germany, powerhouse Portugal, and the highly-ranked Ghana. But it was worth noting the performance of the other CONCACAF teams, as Mexico also made the knockout rounds from a tough group while Costa Rica's exploits were nothing short of sensational. Los Ticos topped a first-round section containing *three* previous World Cup winners in Italy, Uruguay, and England, then beat Greece on penalties to reach the quarterfinal. It was the first time CONCACAF had three representatives in the second round.

The Americans went into the following summer's Gold Cup on the back of two great wins in Europe, 4–3 over Holland and 2–1 against the Germans. But they were friendlies. In the Gold Cup semifinal, they were paired with Jamaica in Atlanta and it should have been a routine victory over the Caribbean island who had plummeted to a world ranking of 113th in 2014. Instead, they were defeated, 2–1, their first home defeat to a Caribbean team since 1969, and to compound the humiliation they lost the third-place playoff to Panama. At the Rose Bowl in Pasadena four months later, Mexico beat them 3–2 in a testy encounter to qualify for the 2017 Confederations Cup in Russia.

By the start of World Cup qualification, in the fall of 2015, Jurgen Klinsmann's four-year reign as coach was at its most tenuous. The USA conceded a goal to St. Vincent and the Grenadines, could only tie in Trinidad & Tobago, and lost to Guatemala—the first time America had not beaten them in almost thirty years. Unbelievably, going into the last match of the round there was a mathematical scenario that a heavy defeat for the States could eliminate them *before* the Hexagonal! The criticism of Klinsmann's player-management and tactical acumen increased.

But a laudable deep run to the Copa America semifinal, a special edition of the tournament featuring ten CONMEBOL countries and six from CONCACAF to celebrate its centennial, reignited the goodwill towards the German. They beat Costa Rica, Paraguay, and Ecuador (Klinsmann picked the same starting lineup for three successive matches—the first time *any* USA coach had selected the same eleven three games running in eighty-six years) to set up a last-four battle with Argentina. Although they were only ninety minutes from the final it may as well have been ninety years, the Lionel Messi-inspired Albiceleste strolling to a 4–0 win. Klinsmann was one of the favorites to be the new England coach in a perfect illustration of how the soccer world had changed: the English wanted a German in charge of their national team despite many Americans thinking he wasn't good enough for theirs!

However, a five-day spell in November signaled his death knell. The Hex opened against Mexico in Columbus and the USA were behind after 20 minutes. They trailed at halftime in a home qualifier for only the second time in thirty years. They lost, 2–1— the first Mexican World Cup triumph on US soil since 1972.

At least it had been a close contest, but the performance in Costa Rica four days later was abysmal and they were run ragged in a 4–0 spanking, their worst qualifying defeat since 1957 and the first time the Americans had ever lost both opening matches in the Hex. It was obvious the team had stopped playing for their coach with reports of confusing and conflicting tactical instructions. Klinsmann, who had feuded with players, Major League Soccer (MLS) commissioner Don Garber, the press, and even the fans, was fired within a week.

Bruce Arena, who had run the team from 1998 to 2006, returned to the helm, a trusted captain to steady the rollicking ship, and qualifying resumed in March with the USA hosting Honduras. Arena picked just five starters from the previous qualifier, already a must-win match three rounds into the Hex. After losing the first two contests it was the greatest challenge the USA had faced in modern qualifying history: how would this fragile, vulnerable team fare against the Honduran shark, circling the flailing body, sensing blood in its neighbor's water? At kickoff, the Americans were pointless at the bottom of the group.

Within five minutes, the crisis was over. The USA was ahead. Half-an-hour in and they were up, 3–0, and coasting, up to fourth in the group. Within 12 seconds of the second half they scored again and it ended 6–0. Crisis? What crisis? It was exactly what was needed, the right game at the right time, against a Honduran side who bumbled their way through the worst exhibition of international defending I have ever seen.

Four days later in the heat of Panama City, the rejuvenated and reenergized USA shared the spoils with their hosts in a 1–1 tie. Clint Dempsey's simple conversion from six yards moved him onto 56 international goals, one behind Landon Donovan's US record. The lead lasted just three minutes though, the still-jittery backline failing to deal with a routine throw-in launched into the penalty area. It was symptomatic of how far expectations had fallen that the Americans were satisfied with avoiding defeat to The Canal Men. They had beaten them in five successive qualifiers and had only lost once in sixteen previous contests.

US Soccer Federation President Sunil Gulati said, "I think we're back on track." The change in coach had improved results—what the British call "the new manager bounce"—but it was still premature to start researching accommodation in Moscow. With a pleasing symmetry, the Americans sat in fourth place with four points after four games, but third spot and automatic qualification remained the goal to avoid the Russian Roulette of a transcontinental playoff.

The next doubleheader in June kicked off with a game against Trinidad & Tobago in Commerce City, Colorado, a stadium picked for two reasons. Firstly, the atmospheric and climatic conditions were as alien as they could possibly be to the Caribbean nation. Despite the loaded home-field advantage, it took a quick-fire double by Christian Pulisic to win the match, 2–0.

The second reason the thin air of Colorado had been selected as the venue was to prepare for the altitude in the Azteca Stadium in Mexico City for the return match against El Tri three days later. Arena sprang a surprise and replaced seven of the starting lineup, even dropping veteran goalkeeper Tim Howard.

It worked. The USA, who had won just once in twenty-three previous attempts in the city, took a stunning lead. Captain Michael Bradley intercepted a pass on the halfway line and the touch took him past two defenders. He spotted the keeper off his line and from 35 yards hit a fabulous audacious chip that sped through the rarefied air and into the net. He was only the sixth American to ever score in the famous venue, and although the hosts equalized, a 1–1 tie and another four points from two games was an acceptable return.

The USA were now up to third with eight points from six matches, a point ahead of Panama. The decision to fire Klinsmann had been vindicated; since the horror show in Costa Rica they had not lost in seven games. The following month they won the Gold Cup, banishing the ghost of their defeat in the previous tournament by defeating Jamaica, 2–1, in the final. Their undefeated run stretched to fourteen matches and the feel-good factor had returned.

Then it left again. Apparently, the feel-good factor was like a rude guest at a Christmas party who breezes by for ten minutes, guzzles all the wine, scoffs all the hors d'oeuvres, flirts with your wife, and then buggers off.

The States lost, 2–0, at home to Costa Rica in September and followed that up with a lucky 1–1 tie in Honduras four days later. At Red Bull Arena in New Jersey it was a victory for Ureña over Arena. Marco Ureña, who plays for San Jose Earthquakes in MLS, scored in each half to give the Ticos a deserved victory. If the USA were to make Russia they would do it by creating history—no American team had lost twice at home in the qualifiers and still made the finals.

The performance in Honduras was worse. Outfought and outplayed, they fell behind after 27 minutes, only equalizing five minutes from time when Bobby Wood got on the end of a goal-mouth scramble after the ball pinballed around the box. But even so, their position was still perilous: with Mexico qualified and Costa Rica a shoo-in, it left Panama, the USA, and Honduras battling for the final slot for Russia with only a single point separating all three teams.

The penultimate match at home to Panama, one point above the USA, looked like being the crucial contest upon which the American dream depended. Little did we know then that the dream was morphing into a nightmare. It was fitting that their last home game in this Mickey Mouse campaign was staged in Orlando.

It was a stroll in the (theme) park. Goals by Pulisic and Wood bookended two from Jozy Altidore and they ran out comfortable, controlled, confident 4–0 victors. Websites published details of our likely seeding for the tournament and images were leaked online of the new uniform for Russia. USA fans breathed a collective sigh of relief as we rubbed our eyes and welcomed, what unfortunately turned out to be, a false dawn.

Christian Pulisic scores the USA's opener against Panama in the qualifier in Orlando, October 2017. The 4–0 win would ultimately be rendered meaningless.

The final round of matches, the culmination of the Hex, the moment when the Americans were set to finally stumble across the line. Honduras vs. Mexico, Panama vs. Costa Rica, Trinidad & Tobago vs. USA. The States had 13 points with a vastly superior goal difference, Panama and Honduras sat on 11 points. If the USA won in the Caribbean they were in. If they tied they were in. Even if they were beaten they were in unless *both* their rivals won.

Trinidad & Tobago were rooted rock-bottom of the group. They had lost eight of their nine matches in the Hex, scoring a total of only five goals. Their coach, Dennis Lawrence, picked a young, inexperienced team with an eye on the next World Cup. The contest was held miles from the capital in the sleepy town of Couva, in a stadium that was mostly empty and ennui-infected. If the Americans had one foot on the plane to Russia, the agreeable Caribbean nation seemed to be pulling them into the cabin and offering them peanuts and a beer.

By halftime, an own goal by Omar Gonzalez and a stunner by Alvin Jones had the USA trailing, 2–0. They were lackluster, lackadaisical, and lifeless. Their saving grace was that both their competitors were also losing, so despite a woeful first half, they were still safe in third place.

Within 90 seconds of the restart, Pulisic (who else?) pulled a goal back. With practically a whole half to play, and the Americans only requiring one goal, it seemed certain they would push on and equalize to seal automatic qualification. But the good news from the islands was tempered by bad news from the mainland. Panama equalized against the already-qualified Ticos and adding insult to injury, TV replays proved it was a ghost goal and that the ball never crossed the line, while Honduras also clawed level in their showdown with Mexico. Still, the States held third spot.

Then with half-an-hour to play, Romell Quioto, signed to Houston Dynamo in MLS, put Honduras 3–2 ahead. They leapfrogged above the USA, who now needed to equalize to move back into the automatic qualification slot. An American goal and they were in. A Panamanian goal and they were out.

And right at the wire, the qualification chickens came home to roost. In the 89th minute in Panama City, defender Román Torres, another MLS star who plies his trade with the Seattle Sounders, rifled a shot into the top corner that earned his country their first World Cup qualification ever. The following morning, the president declared it a national holiday in celebration.

At the full-time whistle in Couva, the Americans collapsed distraught onto the field. They had lost against a country ranked 99th in the world. The biggest soccer-playing country on earth by population, with somewhere in the region of 325 million people, had been eliminated by a nation with a population of 1.3 million—roughly the same as Maine.

Afterwards Michael Bradley described it as the "perfect storm." He said, "Everything that could have possibly gone wrong did, in this stadium and in two other stadiums across the region."

But in truth the seeds of this disaster had been sown long before that night. A qualification campaign spoiled by individual errors, shoddy performances, and questionable tactics. They got what they deserved.

For the first time in thirty-two years, there will be no United States of America at the World Cup.

# CHAPTER THREE

# THE AMERICAN DREAM— USA'S WORLD CUP STORY

The USA holds three World Cup records that can never be broken.

They played the first game. They recorded the first shutout. They notched the first hat trick (if they had scored five minutes earlier they would also hold the record for the first goal).

They also hold a fourth record. In the twenty incarnations of the World Cup, spanning eighty-four years, they are the only nation from outside Europe and South America to finish in the top three.

And it may not be an official record, but a scenario making a player wait *seventy-six years* to score a goal is one of the quirkiest facts the competition has ever seen.

At the first tournament, the USA was one of the four seeded teams along with Uruguay, Brazil, and Argentina. By 1930, soccer was well established in the United States and as far back as 1885 the country was playing internationals against Canada. On June 12, the sixteen players on the roster and their Scottish-born coach Robert "Bob" Millar boarded the SS Munargo in New Jersey for the eighteen-day trip to Montevideo, trainer Jack Coll devising games and exercises to keep up their fitness.

Contrary of popular belief, this squad was not stuffed with nationalized Brits sandbagged in from the Old Country. Five Scottish and one English player had been born across the pond, but all but one had emigrated while very young. The professional career of that player, George Moorhouse, had been limited to two matches for Tranmere Rovers in the bottom tier. This was an outfit raised and coached on American fields, who played for clubs with wonderful names like Holley Carburetor FC, Providence Gold Bugs, Cleveland Slavia, and the New Bedford Whalers. Their imposing stature and physical condition earned them the label "The Shot-Putters."

The USA were in Group 4 with Belgium and Paraguay. Their opening match against the Europeans on July 13 was the first ever played, along with France against Mexico that kicked off simultaneously a few miles away. Frenchman Lucien Laurent scored the first World Cup goal in the 19th minute—four minutes earlier than winger Bart McGhee's strike that put the Americans ahead in their game. They doubled their lead on the stroke of halftime when Tom Florie made it 2–0 and Bert Patenaude scored a third with 21 minutes to go. The first clean sheet in history belonged to goalkeeper Jimmy Douglas.

Four days later, they took on Paraguay and this time were 2–0 ahead within a quarter of an hour thanks to a double from Patenaude, and five minutes after the break he completed his hat trick. That third strike spawned a tale that reached into the next century before finally concluding with a happy ending.

FIFA awarded the second goal to the captain Florie, and so officially the first hat trick in World Cup history belonged to Argentinian Guillermo Stábile, who netted three times forty-eight hours later against Mexico. When Patenaude was inducted into the US Soccer Hall of Fame in 1971 he insisted all three goals were his, although nothing came of it before he died in 1974.

It wasn't until November 2006—more than seventy-six years after the event—that FIFA released a press statement reading, "thanks to evidence from various historians and football fans, as well as lengthy research and confirmation from the US Soccer Federation, American Bert Patenaude has been retrospectively entered in FIFA's records as the first player to score a hat trick in FIFA World Cup history." Better late than never.

The USA were in the semifinal of the inaugural World Cup and would play a rough, tough Argentina who had crushed them, 11–2, at the Olympics two years previously. In light of that, the *New York Times'* headline, "U.S. Favorite to Win World Soccer's Title" seems a trifle optimistic.

In the fourth minute, a crunching tackle on keeper Douglas left him hobbling, shortly after that Ralph Tracy was targeted by another full-bloodied collision that left him a passenger. He continued until halftime but afterwards he was found to have broken his leg, so in the days before substitutes it meant the USA played the vast majority of the contest with nine fit players.

At the break, the Americans were 1–0 behind to a Luis Monti goal (he switched allegiance to Italy and faced the United States again playing for a different country four years later!), and were still in the match at 2–0 down with 21 minutes left. But in the space of 16 minutes Argentina ran riot and notched up another four goals, although Jim Brown slotted home a consolation to make the final result 6–1.

There is a famous World Cup story from this game. It goes that trainer Jack Coll (from Downpatrick, Northern Ireland, incidentally) ran onto the field to treat an injured player but tripped and fell. He landed on his medical bag in which a bottle of chloroform had smashed open and he was overcome by fumes, having to be helped off the field before he had helped the player on it! However, there is no photographic or empirical record of this really happening.

This was the only tournament not to feature a third-place playoff, so both losing semifinalists were awarded bronze medals. However, the FIFA technical report ranks the USA third above Yugoslavia, probably because of their better goal differential record in the group stage.

At the next World Cup, the USA went into the record books again—playing a qualifying game just *three days* before the tournament started!

The United States Football Association (in 1945 they became the US Soccer Football Association, then the US Soccer Federation in 1974), hemmed and hawed over entering the 1934 competition in Italy. While they dithered, Mexico beat Cuba and jumped aboard a ship to Europe, believing—with some justification—that they were the region's representatives.

Then the Americans decided they did want to join the party after all. In a bizarre compromise typical of the befuddled and muddled organization of the time, FIFA had both countries travel to Italy to play a deciding match. So, the teams sailed thousands of miles to another continent for a tournament one of them would not be allowed to play in.

This time the Americans took nineteen players, and the star would be the unknown twenty-six-year-old Aldo "Buff" Donelli, who played college football on Saturdays and soccer on Sundays at Duquesne University in Pennsylvania. He scored for the reserves against the first team in a scrimmage, and played so well in the first half that coach Elmer Schroeder switched him to the firsts at the break. Then he scored for them, equalizing the goal he had scored in the first half! Reportedly veteran Billy Gonsalves threatened to walk out unless Donelli started against Mexico.

It was an astute blackmail. Donelli scored all the goals as the USA ran out 4–2 winners at the pithily named National Stadium of the National Fascist Party in Rome under the gaze of Mussolini and the American ambassador. The Americans had made it to the finals proper and would play the hosts and favorites Italy.

In a single-elimination contest the Italians, who went on to win both the 1934 and 1938 World Cups, trounced the USA, 7–1. Inevitably Donelli scored the consolation. Despite five goals in two games, he never played for the national team again. Instead he became the only person to coach college and professional football simultaneously, in 1941 running both the NFL's Pittsburgh Steelers and Duquesne University. It was fifty-nine years before another American scored four goals in a game (Joe Max-Moore against El Salvador in December 1993).

By the time the next tournament arrived, soccer had stagnated to the extent that the national team had only played three games in four years, all defeats to Mexico in 1937. The USA didn't even bothering entering the 1938 World Cup. They managed a solitary tournament appearance in the following fifty-six years. But it would be a special one.

"The Miracle Match" and "The Game of Their Lives" are two nicknames given to the contest between the USA and England at the Estadio Independencia in the sleepy mountain mining town of Belo Horizonte, Brazil, on June 29, 1950. In arguably the greatest shock in World Cup history the upstart Americans beat the English aristocrats, 1–0. But at the time no one in either country cared.

The apocryphal story is when the score was wired back to London, newspaper editors assumed it was a typing mistake and that England had won, 10–1. There is no proof that ever happened, but England rattling up double figures was plausible: they had recently beaten Italy, 4–0, and Portugal, 10–0. England was ranked the second-best team in the world while the USA had conceded 12 goals to Mexico in two qualifiers and were 500–1 outsiders for the competition.

In their opener, England eased past Chile, 2–0. The USA had taken on Spain and Gino Pariani gave them the lead after 17 minutes but the Europeans hit three goals in the final nine minutes. It was hardly surprising the Americans had run out of steam as they were part-timers in an amateur league who included a hearse driver, a mailman, and a paint stripper.

The legend is that England rested Stanley Matthews, perhaps the best player in the world, to save him for more important games, but he had arrived in Brazil late and missed the first match, so the selectors went with the same lineup who had beaten Chile. Within 90 seconds England had their first attempt on target, by the 12th minute they had already hit the post twice. It appeared the 10,000 spectators would witness a basketball score.

But despite the relentless peppering the American defense was not breached. Then in the 38th minute, Walter Bahr hit a long-range shot that keeper Bert Williams had covered—until up popped dishwasher Joe Gaetjens. The center forward was born in Haiti and represented them in friendlies during World War II and even turned out for them in a qualifier for the following World Cup. He diverted the strike with a diving header, wrong-footing Williams and chalking up the most famous redirect in American soccer history. Ironically he wasn't even a US citizen—under the rules he merely had to declare he *would* apply for citizenship in the future to be eligible. He never did.

The second half was one-way traffic with the ragtag Americans taking the same battering and England pounding away at the defense. However, it was to no avail, and at the final whistle the crowd rushed onto the field to carry off the Americans shoulder

Haitian-born Joe Gaetjens is carried from the field after his deflection defeated England, 1–0, at the 1950 World Cup, the most famous goal in US soccer history.

high. But the seismic score barely registered in either country. There was just one American journalist at the World Cup who had taken vacation and paid his own way, and his report in the *St. Louis Post-Dispatch* was the only coverage in any newspaper. In England, it was barely mentioned in the press as fans cared little about their country's inaugural entry to a tournament thousands of miles away.

In their final game against Chile, the USA were 2–0 behind at halftime, but within three minutes of the restart they tied it up. However, they went on to lose, 5–2, though John Souza had the consolation of making the World Cup All-Star team.

The superhuman effort and the level of grit the Americans drew on to beat England is apparent by their record in the 1950s. They lost twelve out of fifteen matches. Their only wins? Two against Haiti and the victory over England. In the next four matches against the same opponent they were outscored 29–4, a run that included a humiliating 8–1 loss in 1959.

The Joe Gaetjens story had a harrowing, brutal ending after he returned home to the Caribbean island. His two younger brothers were plotting a coup against Haiti dictator Papa Doc Duvalier and, fearing reprisals, the rest of his family fled in 1964. But Gaetjens stayed, believing as he was not involved in politics he would be safe. He was arrested by the notorious Tonton Macoutes secret police and taken to a prison renowned for its inhuman torture. He was never seen again. His body has never been found.

The greatest result in American soccer history was followed by barren decades in the global wilderness. The USA failed to qualify for a World Cup for forty years, a generation of players and fans denied the thrill of a role in the greatest sporting spectacle on earth. It was forty-four years before the USA won another game at the finals. Their tournament pedigree plummet was steep, rapid and long-lasting.

Mexico dominated the region like no other power on any other continent anywhere else on earth. By contrast, the USA did not even record a qualifying win for *eleven years* between beating Haiti in 1954 and Honduras in 1965. In 1973, they lost, 4–0, to Bermuda and were beaten in twelve consecutive games between 1973 and 1975.

However the '70s sowed seeds that would revolutionize the American soccer landscape. The NASL burned briefly but brightly and the newfound passion for the sport ignited an explosion of interest in the game among the country's children. For the first time in generations, youth soccer grabbed a toehold in the nation's consciousness. Some of those kids would represent their country on the world stage.

In 1982 qualifying, the USA finally beat Mexico for the first time in forty-six years with a 2–1 win in Fort Lauderdale in November 1980. They still failed to make it to the finals then or in the next cycle, and if you want an idea of how far the sport's stock had fallen in the country, coach Lothar Osiander was a part-timer who worked in a restaurant. If Joe Gaetjens's goal against England in 1950 is the most famous goal in US soccer history, then Paul Caligiuri's "shot heard around the world" that defeated Trinidad & Tobago to secure a spot at the 1990 finals is perhaps the most important.

The USA was awarded the 1994 tournament and FIFA were under fire for selling out to the Yankee Dollar by taking the event to what was not a traditional soccer nation. If the States had hosted "boasting" just one appearance in the previous sixty years then their credibility would have been rock bottom. The 1990 qualification was paramount to America's standing in the soccer world.

However the Americans' return to the big stage was anti-climatic, drubbed 5–1 by Czechoslovakia and a man sent off in their opening match. The tactics were naive, the team out of their depth, the players rattled. Welcome back to the World Cup, lads.

Four days later in a packed Stadio Olimpico in Rome they battled the hosts Italy. When the Italians scored after 11 minutes it looked like it was going to be a "Christians versus the lions" massacre, but the gladiatorial Americans stayed tight the rest of the match and there were no further goals.

At halftime of their final contest against Austria the match was scoreless, and the Austrians were down to ten men having had a man ejected. But in the second half the wily Europeans scored twice, and although Bruce Murray pulled one back, the USA couldn't find the equalizer. Three games, three defeats. However, more than a dozen players earned transfers to professional clubs, the Americans had reintroduced themselves to the world, and the stage fright had been conquered.

Every host nation expects to do well on the field. The USA, in 1994 the only hosts in history without a professional league, set records off it. Colossal crowds flocked to matches across the nation.

The USA chalked up more World Cup history as their opener against Switzerland in Detroit's Pontiac Silverdome was the first to be played indoors. The Americans, now under experienced Serbian coach Bora Milutinović, were nerveless in their home-nation debut. They fell behind six minutes before the break but, unlike the previous tournament, they didn't wilt and equalized within five minutes. It finished 1–1.

Their next game against the fancied Colombians is infamous for what happened nine days later on another continent. The deadly consequence understandably overshadows a tremendous performance.

In front of almost 94,000 fans at the Rose Bowl they went ahead when a cross into the box was deflected into his own goal by defender Andres Escobar. In the second half they doubled their lead, and although Colombia pulled one back at the end it was too little, too late. When Escobar returned home to Medellín he argued with three men at 3 a.m. in a nightclub parking lot and was shot six times. He bled to death and a member of one of the town's drug cartels confessed to the killing.

After a wait one week shy of forty-four years, the USA finally had another win at the World Cup.

They could not repeat their heroics in their final group match against Romania and lost 1–0, but four points from a win and a tie saw them into the knockout stage as one of the best third-place teams. For the first time since the inaugural tournament, the USA advanced in the World Cup.

In the last 16, on Independence Day, they faced the favorites Brazil. Roared on by a passionate support, the Americans' disciplined, determined display frustrated the Samba Boys. Two minutes before halftime, Brazilian defender Leonardo jammed his elbow into Tab Ramos's head, fracturing the American's skull. He was red-carded and the South Americans had to negotiate the second half in the scorching heat of Stanford Stadium a man short. Could the Americans pull off a shock to rival 1950?

No. Bebeto put Brazil in front and any chance the USA had of scrambling an equalizer went when Fernando Clavijo was also dismissed. Still, on the field the Americans had won respect, off it their commercial acumen set a new benchmark for the tournament. Soccer was (re) Born in the USA.

Unfortunately, as wildly successful as 1994 had been, 1998 saw the USA crash back to earth.

The 1998 tournament, racked with infighting and disunity, was their least successful in eighty-four years of the World Cup— three defeats and a single goal scored. Even more disappointing was the maelstrom of backbiting and negativity surrounding the squad and staff.

Steve Sampson was promoted from assistant to replace Milutinović and became the first full-time American-born coach. Shockingly, he left captain John Harkes—whom he had lauded just two years previously as "captain for life"—out of the squad. He offered the vague explanation it was down to "leadership issues," but in 2010 he admitted it was because Harkes was having an affair with teammate Eric Wynalda's wife. In a swipe at Sampson, Harkes titled his autobiography, *Captain for Life: And Other Temporary Assignments*.

The United States were drawn in the so-called Group of Death, not labeled thus because of the strength of the teams but due to the clashes of political ideologies: the USA, Germany, Yugoslavia, and Iran. Their match against Iran was nicknamed the "Mother of All Matches," while the USA had been integral in NATO's role in the Balkan conflict (the Serbian capital Belgrade would be bombed the following year).

The Americans lost their opening contest, 2–0, to Germany (future USA coach Jurgen Klinsmann scored the second goal) and then faced Iran. Despite press attempts to ratchet up the tension before the Islamic state took on their Great Satan, both sets of players mingled before and after the showdown with no hint of trouble.

Although the USA hit the woodwork twice, they fell 2–0 behind to rapier counterattacks in each half. A late Brian McBride strike set up a frantic finish but the USA were knocked out two games in. The Iranians celebrated as though they had won the tournament and in parts of America, rejoicing emigrants took to the streets. The USA then lost, 1–0, to Yugoslavia and were ranked rock bottom of the thirty-two finalists. Within 100 hours Sampson resigned and was replaced by Bruce Arena.

From the sublime to the ridiculous—their worst performance at the finals was followed by their best.

Third place in 1930 is officially the best finish, but only a dozen other countries entered and two wins was enough to secure the bronze. The thrilling run to the quarterfinals in 2002 included the scalps of storied, experienced nations, and but for a blatant, outrageous act of cheating by the Germans in the last eight, the USA may well have made the semifinal.

It was an unkind draw that landed the USA with hosts South Korea, Portugal, and Poland. The Poles were tournament perennials, the Koreans had been preparing for five months, Portugal were ranked fifth in the world. The Europeans were expected to advance to the knockout stage comfortably. Both lost their opening games.

A day after the co-hosts beat Poland, 2–0, the Americans lined up against Portugal's Golden Generation, and in an astonishing 36 minutes swept into a 3–0 lead. I have a Portuguese stepfather and I watched open-mouthed, disbelieving the unfolding drama. It was the most intense, overwhelming, devastating American performance against top-class opposition I've ever seen.

It was the first time the USA scored three goals in a World Cup match in seventy-two years. The shell-shocked Europeans pulled one back six minutes before the break and another goal with 20 minutes left set up a nervy finale, but the Americans hung on. The result rivaled that of beating England in 1950.

Next they lined up against the Koreans in front of a rowdy home crowd, and thanks to goalkeeper Brad Friedel's penalty-kick save they escaped with a 1–1 tie. When Portugal dismantled Poland, 4–0, a few hours later it meant the USA needed to avoid defeat against the Eastern Europeans to make the knockout rounds.

Poland were out of the competition but powered into a 2–0 lead in the first five minutes. Although Friedel saved another penalty the USA lost, 3–1, and looked to be on their way home. But although a manufactured tie between Portugal and South Korea would have seen both teams progress, Portugal had a player sent off after less than half an hour and then had a second kicked out in the 66th minute. The Koreans scored against the nine men and that strike saw the USA into the last 16. They would face their old foes, Mexico.

A vital early goal from Brian McBride, three fabulous saves by Friedel, and a Landon Donovan header made it 2–0. The match became increasingly bad tempered and five players from each side were booked while Mexican captain Rafael Marquez was shown a straight red card. The Americans were in a World Cup quarterfinal against Germany.

The Germans were far from a classic Panzer-like outfit who were rampaging through an unarmored field, and the USA, their confidence sky-high, fancied their chances against an unusually erratic and misfiring opponent. Alas it was not to be. Germany's outstanding midfielder Michael Ballack scored the winner but it was goalkeeper Oliver Kahn who won them the match. Kahn—voted not only the tournament's best keeper but the best overall player—made a string of saves to deny the US, leading the German newspaper *Süddeutsche Zeitung* to describe the team's formation as "a flat back one."

The crucial save, however, belonged to Torsten Frings, the midfielder's handball on the goal line preventing Gregg Berhalter's shot from hitting the back of the net. The infraction was missed by Scottish referee Hugh Dallas.

Claudio Reyna became the third American named to the team of the tournament (after Patenaude in 1930 and Souza in 1950) and Landon Donovan was crowned Best Young Player. Of course, the problem with improved performance is increased expectation.

The USA were a dizzying fifth in the FIFA world ranking for the 2006 tournament. (The ridiculous formula used to compile the monthly chart has since been amended; Germany were rated 19th at the same time.) The quarterfinal run in 2002, the stroll through CONCACAF qualifying, the Gold Cup triumph in 2005 combined to fuel a wave of optimism and hype. You know where this is going.

The Americans faced another Group of Death containing Italy, the Czech Republic, and Ghana. By halftime of their opener against the Czechs, they were 2–0 down. A third with 15 minutes left and the American soccer bubble had been well and truly burst. The gap between the game management and tactical awareness of the two sides was pronounced, the USA floundering and frantically kicking to stay afloat while the Czechs coasted, barely breaking a sweat.

Next up was Italy—but this time the Americans surprised the world with an energetic display in an extraordinary, enthralling match. The Italians took the lead midway through the first half but the US leveled through an own goal. Seconds later Daniele De Rossi was shown a straight red card for smashing his elbow into Brian McBride's face: with the score tied and a man advantage, the USA were set to sneak an unlikely win.

But in two crazy minutes either side of halftime, Pablo Mastroeni was sent off for a reckless tackle and Eddie Pope joined him in the locker room after receiving two yellow cards. From being a man up they were now down to nine players, only the fourth game in tournament history with three dismissals. But somehow the Americans held out to earn their first World Cup point in Europe.

In the final group match against Ghana the Africans took the lead but Clint Dempsey equalized before, yet again, tactical naivete and inexperience led to them conceding a needless penalty kick in first-half injury time. They went into the locker room with the psychological blow of being 2–1 behind: they hit the post in the second half but it was a limp, tepid performance considering the stakes.

They had managed a total of four shots on target in three games. For the second time in three World Cups, the USA were officially ranked at the bottom. By the end of the year, coach Arena had gone and the US had dropped out of the world's top 30.

Bob Bradley was in charge for 2010 and, for once, the draw was kind to the USA in two respects: the strength of the teams and a high-profile clash for the fans. The group featured Algeria, Slovenia, and England and *The Sun* newspaper in London, my old employers, splashed this on their front page:

England
Algeria
Slovenia
Yanks

The buildup to the opening match against England was dominated by memories of the famous 1950 clash. This time, though, the Americans conceded after only four minutes, but they refused to be bulldozed and after they weathered the initial flurry, the English ran out of steam. Five minutes before the break, Dempsey's speculative long-distance shot squirmed into the net and the contest ended 1–1. The *New York Post*'s front page read, "USA WINS 1–1. Greatest tie against the British since Bunker Hill."

Against Slovenia it seemed the USA were determined to make things as difficult for themselves as possible and went in at the break 2–0 behind. But they rallied after the interval, Donovan halved the deficit and eight minutes from time the coach's son, Michael Bradley, made it 2–2. The comeback tie felt like a win, and for only the second time since 1930 the USA were unbeaten after two games. They were well-placed to make the next round— as always though, there were twists and turns ahead.

They bossed the match against Algeria needing a win to make the last 16 but couldn't find a way through, hitting the bar, missing two sitters, and having a goal ruled out for offside. But in injury time it was the dynamic double D duo, Dempsey and Donovan, to the rescue again: Dempsey's shot was blocked and Donovan converted the rebound. They held on for the nail-biting, heart-stopping final minutes and won their first-round group for the first time since 1930. I was emailed a new Americanized version of that front-page headline:

Yanks
England
Slovenia

Their reward was a last-16 game with Ghana, who had eliminated them in the previous tournament. It was the most-watched soccer game in American history with viewing figures close to 20 million. Unfortunately, the broadcast turned out to be a rerun.

The Americans, hellbent on gift-wrapping their opponents a head start, fell behind early for the third time in four matches. But just after an hour—once more—the dynamic duo combined, Dempsey winning a penalty converted by Donovan. Extra-time. The USA insisted on playing catch-up and presented their customary early goal start to the Africans. It was enough to see Ghana into the quarterfinals.

For only the third time since 1930, the USA had progressed to the knockout stage, and the disappointment at the sense of a chance missed was indicative of how far the team had come. The higher standards led to Bradley's firing a year later.

If we have learned anything from our examination of the USA's eighty-four years of World Cup history, it is that things are never dull. For a country that has missed half the tournaments the amount of drama and shocks they have been involved in is ridiculous. The Yanks are the crazy cousin of world soccer, the relative you only see at family reunions but who always has a story to tell and turns up married to a Romanian juggler, holding a monkey dressed as a butler.

We finish with the most recent competition in Brazil. Almost 200,000 fans in the USA bought tickets, more than England, Germany, and Argentina combined. A year before the competition coach Jurgen Klinsmann led the States to a twelve-match winning streak that included lifting the Gold Cup and a victory over Germany, but his bombshell to leave behind record goal-scorer Donovan split the players, the staff, and the fans.

There is no doubt the USA has had a disproportional share of tough round-one groups. That was continued—magnified—

in Brazil when they were drawn with Germany, Portugal, and Ghana. It was the nightmare scenario of drawing the world's second-best team (Germany) and the fourth-best (Portugal) according to FIFA's official rankings, while the Africans had eliminated the States in the two previous World Cups.

But in my newspaper column I predicted the Americans would finish above Portugal, chronic under-performers. They had qualified from Northern Ireland's section and we had endured a horrendously embarrassing campaign, failing to beat Luxembourg at home, losing to them away, and winning just once in ten matches. Yet, we tied in Portugal, the home team only equalizing 11 minutes from the end, and we had also been 2–1 ahead in Belfast until we had a man sent off. No way were they the fourth-best team on the planet.

Indeed Germany pummeled Portugal, 4–0, in the opening game, the heavy defeat a potentially fatal blow to their goal difference. And just 30 seconds into their opener things looked even better for the USA when Dempsey scored the fifth-fastest goal in World Cup history against Ghana. In the 82nd minute the Africans tied it up, but the now customary twist in the tale was yet to unfurl, and with four minutes left, substitute John Brooks, the unlikeliest of heroes, popped up to head in the winner. He was the first American sub to score in the finals, Dempsey the first to hit the back of the net in three World Cups, DaMarcus Beasley the first to play in four.

Next up was a wounded Portugal with one of the all-time greats Cristiano Ronaldo, under immense pressure after their spanking by the Germans. Within five minutes the Americans remembered they were supposed to concede a silly early goal and they went 1–0 down.

But in a fantastic slugfest full of end-to-end action, Jermaine Jones tied it up, and when Dempsey made it 2–1 with nine minutes to go it looked like the Americans were through to the last 16. But, as you know, the unexpected is not only likely but mandatory: in the *fifth* minute of injury time, that man Ronaldo curled in an exquisite, delectable peach of a cross that Varela converted. Four points from two games was a great return, but the last-gasp tie felt like a crushing defeat.

So a tie between the USA and Germany would put both teams into the next round. The USA had a German coach—one who had scored against the USA in the 1998 tournament. But if Ghana beat Portugal and the USA lost, then goal difference would decide who stayed on.

Ten minutes into the second half, Germany took the lead while Ghana and Portugal were tied at 1–1. If Ghana scored again they would leapfrog the Americans on goals scored. Unbearable tension. Two simultaneous kickoffs, progression to the knockout stage balanced on a knife-edge. One ghastly mistake or one inspired flash of genius would decide it.

With 10 minutes left Ronaldo scored for Portugal. Ghana needed to strike twice to qualify. The American nation breathed a wee touch easier, and despite the 1–0 defeat, they made it through.

In the second round, the USA faced Belgium, a group not so much sprinkled with star power as doused, bathed, and showered in it, with more than half their squad sparkling in England's Premier League. Around 21 million Americans tuned in for the shootout—which resembled a literal shootout between keeper Tim Howard and the Belgian attack. Time and time again he foiled them, recording a World Cup-record 15 saves, and at full-time the match remained goalless.

Goalkeeper Tim Howard in action during his heroic performance against Belgium in the last 16 at the 2014 World Cup in Brazil.

Three minutes into extra time he was finally beaten, and by halftime in extra time it was 2–0. Within two minutes, teenage substitute Julian Green's goal gave the Americans hope, but Belgium held out for the win. Howard's heroics in goal made him an overnight sensation, receiving a call from President Obama and spawning a slew of internet memes, "Things Tim Howard Could Save" such as the Titanic.

For the first time the USA had made it to the knockout stages of successive World Cups. The ghost of those forty lost years between 1950 and 1990 had been well and truly laid to rest.

Let's hope 2018 does not signal the start of another four decades of the USA wandering in the soccer wilderness.

# CHAPTER FOUR

# THE STARTLING ELEVEN

World Cup history is stacked with saints and sinners, heroes and villains, gentlemen and cheats. Off-field shenanigans. On-field play-acting. Dastardly deeds and dirty tricks. Misunderstandings from a loss in translation. Confusing cultural clashes. Nations from around the globe have battled on five different continents in a combustible potion that stretches from the interwar years to the Internet age. Some events unfolded as farce, others as tragedy, a few are curiosities which enriched the narrative of the greatest sporting event on Earth. Let's take a look at some memorable moments from past tournaments.

## 1934: Luis Monti plays in successive World Cup finals—for two different teams!

Nationality is tricky. For instance, I have three passports: I'm from Northern Ireland, part of the United Kingdom, so I'm British. However I was born on the island of Ireland so I'm entitled to a Republic of Ireland passport as well, while in 2007 I took

American citizenship. So although I reluctantly admit my dream of playing international soccer has gone, at least if I did sit by the phone every day waiting for a call-up I have increased my chances threefold.

At both the 2010 and 2014 World Cups the same two brothers lined up on opposing teams as they chose to represent different countries. The Boateng half-brothers were born in Berlin to a Ghanaian father, Jerome opting for Germany while Kevin-Prince turned out for Ghana.

FIFA allows players to change allegiance between nations even after they have played internationals, as long as they were only exhibitions and not competitive matches. American stalwart Jermaine Jones was born in Frankfurt to a US soldier, and represented Germany three times before switching to the US Men's National Team. But no one will ever match the remarkable feat of Luis Monti.

Monti was an all-action Argentinean midfielder who won the league four times with two different teams and was nicknamed "Double Wide" because of his hulking size. At the 1930 World Cup he scored against both France and the United States as the Albiceleste reached the final, losing 4–2 to hosts Uruguay.

After the tournament Monti signed for Italian powerhouse Juventus and helped them win four consecutive championships, but sixteen months after the last of his 16 caps for Argentina he made his debut for Italy against Hungary. He went on to make 18 appearances for the Azzurri and took part in every game for them at the 1934 World Cup. After defeating Czechoslovakia, 2–1, in the final he lifted the trophy with his new country—and he was voted into the Team of the Tournament in both 1930 and 1934 with two different nations!

## 1962—The Battle of Santiago

Certain clips in sporting history are enriched by commentary as famous as the event. That is the case with this first-round match between Italy and hosts Chile, in which BBC presenter David Coleman welcomes the viewer with the introduction:

"The game you are about to see is the most stupid, appalling, disgusting and disgraceful exhibition of football, possibly in the history of the game . . . this is the first time these two countries have met—we hope it will be the last."

If you listen to his remarks during the game (there is a four-minute clip on YouTube), he is equal parts baffled and outraged. Obviously covering soccer in austere postwar England with its sense of decency and fair play left him totally unqualified to report on the carnage unraveling before him.

Bizarrely, the bad blood started when two Italian journalists criticized the host's population and infrastructure, calling Santiago a rundown den of inequity where, "taxis are as rare as faithful husbands." The Chilean press hit back and labeled the Italians oversexed fascists. The seething atmosphere on the terraces inevitably spilled over onto the pitch—what was surprising was that it happened so fast.

English referee Ken Aston, who invented the yellow and red cards still used today, gave the first foul 12 seconds after kickoff.

By the eighth minute he had sent off Italian Giorgio Ferrini, who refused to go. A police squad marched onto the field to drag him away. It took 10 minutes to remove him. Already Coleman was calling the contest, "The most stupid, incredible spectacle I've ever seen anywhere in the world."

Italian forward Giorgio Ferrini is escorted off the field by police after being sent off by English referee Ken Aston eight minutes after kick-off in the Battle of Santiago, Chile 1962.

Next Chile's Leonel Sánchez, the son of a professional fighter, laid out Mario David with a punch. Coleman, also a boxing commentator, said, "That was one of the neatest left hooks I've ever seen."

Minutes later, David took revenge and cracked his opponent in the head with a flying kick. He was dismissed and Italy were two men down. Coleman, struggling for superlatives, described it as, "One of the most cold-blooded and lethal tackles I've ever seen." As coaches, substitutes, and staff invaded the field, David sneaked back on. Aston spotted him and escorted him off for a second time.

Chile won, 2–0, after escaping censure for challenges ranging from niggling to outrageous, but by then the contest had descended into a cage fight punctuated by a running battle of provocation, slapping, kicking, and spitting. Italy's Humberto Maschio had his nose broken by a punch (Sánchez again) and the cops intervened another three times to regain control.

Afterwards, Aston complained his inexperienced assistants, a Mexican official, and the Israeli Leo Goldstein had been out of their depth (Goldstein had been on his way to the gas chamber when a Nazi asked if anyone wanted to referee a soccer game, he volunteered, survived the war, and emigrated to the States, making it into the National Soccer Hall of Fame). He said, "I wasn't reffing a football match, I was acting as an umpire in military maneuvers."

## 1966: The World Cup is stolen

The Jules Rimet trophy was stolen from a stamp exhibition weeks before the 1966 World Cup kicked off. It was later found by a dog named Pickles.

It's incredible to imagine it now, but the lackadaisical way the most famous sporting prize on Earth was looked after is spectacularly ramshackle even by the hippy-trippy-anything-goes standards of the sixties. It was on display at the Stampax show in Westminster Central Hall, and to give you an idea of the amateurish level of this whole escapade, the hall was closed on Sundays to hold church services on the floor below. In addition, the guard stationed closest to the trophy was given the day off.

A burglar removed the screws from the back door, pried off the padlock on the glass case, and waltzed back out the way he came. Hardly a *Mission Impossible*-style heist months in the planning requiring high-tech gadgetry and death-defying stunts. A better-informed thief would have swiped the unattended rare stamps worth millions of pounds.

The eyewitness accounts of a suspicious man in the vicinity were so comically varied (he was tall, he was short, etc.) that the police amalgamated them all into one, thus appealing to the public to look for someone no one had described.

The next day, Football Association chairman Joe Mears received a package containing the removable lining from the trophy and a demand for 15,000 pounds. He contacted the police, who filled a suitcase with a fake ransom payment of bundles of newspaper with real bills on top, and a detective went to the handover in Battersea Park.

The "kidnapper" failed to notice he was handed a suitcase of paper and got in the policeman's car to lead him to the trophy, but he spotted a trailing undercover vehicle and jumped out. He was captured and turned out to be Edward Betchley, a petty thief with a criminal record that included receiving stolen tins of corned beef. He served two years in jail.

A week later, David Corbett took four-year-old Pickles on a walk. The black-and-white collie sniffed at a parcel under a neighbor's car that was wrapped in newspaper and tied with string. Corbett opened it, recognized the trophy, and handed it into his local police station. When he told the officer he had found the World Cup, he said the response was, "Doesn't look very World Cuppy to me."

Pickles was an overnight worldwide sensation, starring in TV shows, a movie, and attending the celebration banquet when the hosts won the tournament. His inquisitive nose brought his owner various rewards of thousands of pounds, enough money then to buy a house in a leafy London suburb (much more than the players who won the trophy that summer). Tragically he hung himself the following year when his chain leash caught on a tree branch while chasing a cat. He was buried in the back garden and his collar is on display in the National Football Museum in Manchester.

## 1970: World Cup-winning captain Bobby Moore is arrested

If David Beckham was accused of stealing jewelry from a hotel gift shop you would dismiss it as a publicity stunt or bribery attempt. England captain Bobby Moore was not so lucky when he was snared in this tawdry affair.

Moore and his wife Tina were the Posh and Becks of their day (a contemporary *New York Times* report called him, "The Golden Boy of British soccer;" famously Beckham was known as Golden Balls by his wife). He was an outstanding graceful defender and his 108 appearances for his country was an outfield record until it was broken, ironically enough, by Beckham. As England jetted to South America in May 1970 to defend their title, he was twenty-nine and at the peak of his career.

The squad checked into the Hotel Tequendama in Bogotá two days before a friendly against Colombia, and that evening Moore and midfielder Bobby Charlton browsed in the Fuego Verde (Green Fire) jewelry store in the lobby. They left without buying anything.

As they stood in the foyer, the shop assistant approached and accused them of stealing a diamond-and-emerald bracelet. The players denied it and offered to be searched, and when they both gave statements to the police it appeared to be the end of the matter. After a 4–0 win the party flew onto Quito to play Ecuador.

However, in what would turn out to be an important detail, their flight from Ecuador to Mexico City was routed back through Bogotá with a four-and-a-half-hour layover. They checked back into the same hotel and two detectives arrested Moore for theft.

A new witness had come forward who claimed he watched through a window as Moore stole the item. The team left for Mexico while Moore was put under house arrest at the home of the director of the Colombian Football Federation. The news caused pandemonium in England as the nation faced the prospect of losing their captain and linchpin for their defense of the World Cup. British Prime Minister Harold Wilson ordered diplomatic pressure to be exerted on the Colombian government.

The judge ordered a reenactment and the worker's eyewitness testimony was proven to be false. Moore was released due to lack of evidence and three months later Bogotá's chief of police announced Moore had been the victim of an attempted setup, and that the new witness had been bribed by the store owner.

Moore went on to play in the US for the San Antonio Thunder and the Seattle Sounders in the late '70s, and eight times for the Carolina Lightnin' in 1983, before dying from cancer at age fifty-one in 1993.

## 1974: Germany beats . . . Germany

It was the physical manifestation of the ideological struggle raging in Europe, a battle that brought heat to the Cold War that figuratively and literally had divided the continent. For the only time in the four decades of their existence, East and West Germany met on a soccer field.

The 1974 World Cup was staged in an era when terrorism was rife, hijackings rampant, and political extremism everywhere. The host nation had been the site of the 1972 massacre at the Munich Olympics and there were tanks on the airport runways, police patrolling the terraces, body searches at the stadiums.

The Soviet Union occupied East Germany (officially named the German Democratic Republic with a wonderful lack of irony) after World War II and ran it from the divided city of Berlin until Germany was reunified in 1990. The only time they qualified for the World Cup was, inevitably, when it was staged by their neighbors. It seemed preordained they would be pitted together in the same first-round group.

Both teams were already through to the second stage before the showdown at Hamburg's Volksparkstadion, with the West, the reigning European champions, overwhelming favorites to defeat an opponent known as "the little brother." With the maelstrom of doctrines and the combustible tinderbox of politics swirling around the contest—and the security forces' helicopter circling above the field—the East let around 1,500 (regime-vetted) fans cross the Iron Curtain to attend.

A cagey game with few opportunities made it appear both sides were settling for a scoreless tie, but with 12 minutes to go, Jürgen Sparwasser received a cross around 20 yards from the West German goal. He slotted the ball past legendary goalkeeper Sepp Maier who did his part for cross-border relations by collapsing facedown before the midfielder even shot. The political tensions meant the players were even banned from swapping shirts after the match.

The communist state celebrated a propaganda-rich victory, although in a delicious twist, scorer Sparwasser defected to the

West in the late '80s while playing in a veterans' competition. But West German captain Franz Beckenbauer believed the defeat provided the spark that led to them winning the trophy—"it woke us up" as he put it.

Even when the Germans lose at the World Cup they still manage to win!

## 1982: Arab prince forces the referee to disallow a goal

One of my favorite footnotes in World Cup history is the day an Arabian ruler ordered his country's team to leave the field unless the referee changed his mind about a decision. I love the incident because the threat worked. The prince's intervention led to the official wiping out a perfectly good goal.

The man in question was Prince Fahad of Kuwait, brother of the Gulf state's emir. Kuwait had reached their first finals and reportedly every member of the squad had been awarded a Cadillac, a house, a piece of land, and a speedboat by the ruling family. They were trailing France, 3–1, in their second game when diminutive midfielder Alain Giresse received the ball on the edge of the Arabs' penalty area. A whistle shrilled and the nearest Kuwaiti defender stopped, thinking it had been blown by the referee. Giresse blasted the ball into the net and the Soviet referee, Miroslav Stupar, signaled for a goal. But the whistle had come from the crowd.

Prince Fahad, who was also the Kuwaiti Football Association president, waved at the players to leave the field. The match paused as coach Carlos Alberto Parreira (who would lead his native Brazil to World Cup triumph in 1994) tried to find out what he wanted them to do. After a few minutes of signaling back and forth, Prince Fahad left his seat in the stand and stormed onto the field to remonstrate with Stupar. Whatever persuasive language he used worked—Stupar disallowed the goal and restarted play with a drop ball. The French were furious, and a second protest erupted as their apoplectic coach, Michel Hidalgo, demanded the goal be reinstated. He was restrained by police, who were now blanketing the field.

France scored a fourth anyway in the 89th minute while Stupar never took charge of another international. Prince Fahad was fined the (not) princely sum of 8,000 pounds. He died in 1990 defending Dasman Palace against the invading Iraqi forces in the first Gulf War.

## 1982: Anschluss!

The matchup between West Germany and Austria in 1982 changed the format of soccer tournaments forever. But FIFA couldn't say that they hadn't been warned.

The scheduling at the previous World Cup had Argentina going into their crucial contest with Peru knowing they needed victory by four goals to reach the final. They won, 6–0. But after fifty-two years of World Cups, FIFA had still not worked out that all final games in a round-robin stage should start simultaneously.

Group 2 in Spain contained West Germany, Austria, Chile, and debutantes Algeria. The Africans had shocked the world by defeating the Germans—the reigning European Champions—in the first game. The Germans' overconfident coach, Jupp Derwall, confessed he had not even shown the squad a video of the Algerians because he thought they would laugh at him. The Africans then beat the South Americans as well.

The final match was Germany against Austria in Gijon 24 hours after Algeria played Chile. If the Germans beat Austria, the three countries would be level on four points and goal difference would be used to separate them. A win for Germany by one or two goals would see both them and Austria safely through to the next round.

Germany won, 1–0. Shocker. The result that suited both countries is known as The Disgrace of Gijon.

Horst Hrubesch scored after 10 minutes. There was not a single shot on target in the second half. The teams' nonchalance is reminiscent of fathers playing with toddlers in the garden rather than a crucial World Cup match. In Germany and Austria they call it Nichtangriffspakt von Gijón (Non-aggression pact of Gijón), while it is also known as the Anschluss, the name given to the two nations' unification in 1938.

There was universal outrage. German broadcasters stopped commentating in disgust, Austrian TV advised their watchers to switch off, and the local Spanish newspaper printed the game report in their crime section. The French coach suggested the two countries be awarded the Nobel Peace Prize. Both teams were unrepentant and defiant. "We wanted to progress, not play football," said Derwall.

Algeria protested to FIFA, but unpalatable as it was, technically no rules had been broken. These days, the final round of games kick off at the same time, a direct result of the storm of controversy brewed up by the Disgrace of Gijon.

## 1986: The Hand of God

While the Disgrace of Gijon was mired in a gray area between legality and illegality, there was never any doubt about the Hand of God—a sneaky, sly, unlawful act of deception that Diego Maradona got away with.

The England vs. Argentina quarterfinal at the 1986 World Cup was loaded with emotion before a ball was kicked (or punched) as it was just four years after the Falklands War. Argentina had invaded the British islands off its coast and the UK retook the territory with the Argentinians surrendering humiliatingly quickly, but not before the conflict left around 1,000 dead.

The match was scoreless at halftime in the humidity-drenched high altitude of Mexico City's famous Azteca Stadium. Six

Argentina's captain Diego Maradona opens the scoring against English goalkeeper Peter Shilton in the 1986 quarterfinal with help from "The Hand of God."

minutes after the restart, Maradona jinked past three opponents and laid the ball off, but it was intercepted by Steve Hodge, who sliced his clearance and it skied backwards. Maradona jumped for it ahead of onrushing goalkeeper Peter Shilton and punched the ball into the net.

Shilton confronted the Tunisian referee and other teammates chased the official as he ran back to the halfway line. Watch the video and you see a guilty 5-foot-5 Maradona swivel around to see if he got away with not using his head—at least not literally—to outjump the keeper with an eight-inch height advantage.

Four minutes later, Maradona collected the ball in his own half and accelerated on a mazy 60-yard shimmy that left half the English team chasing shadows. For his final flourish, he bamboozled Shilton with a dummy to leave him sitting on the ground. It is regularly voted the greatest goal of all time. Argentina won, 2–1, and in Buenos Aires they celebrated the result as revenge for the Falklands.

Afterwards Maradona said his first goal had been scored, "A little with the head of Maradona and a little with the hand of God."

Steve Hodge, the midfielder who skewed the ball back to Maradona, swapped shirts with him after the match. When Hodge appeared with the jersey on a British soccer show in the '90s, I noticed the number 10 on Maradona's jersey was an unusual silver color. I discovered why while researching this book.

The Argentineans had complained that their cotton uniforms were too heavy but their official supplier could not replace them in time. So a coach bought new outfits from a local backstreet sports store and they had the association's emblem sewn onto them.

Those silver digits? They were American football numbers. The shirt is now on display in England's National Football Museum.

## 1998: Ronaldo does the hokey cokey

This is the final memorable not for what happened on the field but what went on before kickoff. The Brazilian superstar was in, then he was out, then he was in again.

Ronaldo, nicknamed "The Phenomenon," was a player with power and pace at the peak of his physical prowess. He was the two-time reigning World Player of the Year and on the run to the championship match against the hosts France he had scored four goals and assisted on three more.

But when the lineup was handed to officials, Ronaldo's name was missing.

Rabid speculation exploded on TV screens around the globe with murmurings from the team hotel filtering into the press box that he had suffered a fit. But then an updated team sheet, handed to the referee shortly before kickoff, had him back in. Broadcasters, commentators, and analysts were as baffled as the viewers.

With the world holding its breath, the greatest player on the planet walked onto the field for the biggest game on Earth. But he was subdued and under-par, lacking his explosive speed or devastating dribbling ability. Brazil were beaten, 3–0, the first time they had ever lost a World Cup final (the defeat to Uruguay in 1950 was the final round-robin match).

A government inquiry discovered that while resting in his room he suffered a violent fit during which he foamed at the mouth and shook uncontrollably, an unprecedented seizure likely triggered by stress. He was taken to a clinic for tests, but after being given the all-clear he rushed to the stadium and arrived 40 minutes before the start. He insisted he was well and begged coach Mario Zagallo to reinstate him, which he did.

If Zagallo had left out Ronaldo when he was cleared by doctors, he would have been damned. Instead he was damned for playing him just hours after suffering a fit. Ronaldo still was voted the tournament's best player.

## 2006: Zizou's headbutt

When France won the 1998 World Cup they projected the face of Zinedine Zidane, the team talisman, onto the Arc de Triomphe. The iconic landmark had long been the site of patriotic ceremonies, and now it displayed a son of Algerian immigrants with an Arab name.

In his next final he dominated the headlines for a different reason—the most famous headbutt in sporting history.

The showdown at Berlin's Olympic Stadium pivoted around two protagonists: Zidane and Inter Milan center back Marco Materazzi. After seven minutes, Materazzi gave away a penalty kick and it was Zidane who converted it to put Les Bleus ahead. The lead lasted 12 minutes before Italy equalized with a header from a corner. Guess who scored? Yep, Materazzi.

With two quick goals it was a curiously sparkling open game, but after the early exciting flurry it petered out and ground into extra time. With 10 minutes left before penalty kicks, Zidane was sent off after he snapped and smacked his head into Materazzi's chest when the Italian taunted him.

France's spot kick expert had scored penalties both in the semifinal and the final, but with him in the locker room they were a designated player short for the shootout. They lost when David Trezeguet missed. Of course, Materazzi scored his.

The Argentinian referee had missed the off-the-ball incident and the fourth official alerted him to it. Zidane's great contradiction was that a maestro with such grace, elegance, and serenity on the ball was capable of petulant violence. He is one of only two players ever red-carded in different World Cups. It was the fourteenth ejection of his career; a round dozen came for retaliation to provocation. The thirty-four-year-old never played again.

More than a year later, Materazzi revealed what had happened. The Italian had pulled Zidane's jersey and the Frenchman, fed up with the close attention from the 6-foot-4 defender, said to him in response to yet another tug, "If you want my shirt, I will give it to you afterwards."

Materazzi responded, "I prefer the whore that is your sister."

## 2010: The French implode

Despite Zizou's moment of madness in the most critical soccer event on the planet, he was forgiven by the French people. If he had not thrown his head up (or more accurately, down) and stayed on the field, maybe his penalty kick expertise would have won the trophy. But it was a glittering career barely besmirched by his crazy curtain call.

When the 2010 squad returned home, however, it was a different story.

It was an unhappy camp from the get-go with reports that senior players disliked coach Raymond Domenech and that they were dismissive of his tactics. It was a roster often sullen and uncooperative, riddled with cliques and divisions.

They started with a dreary goalless tie against a Uruguay side who had been reduced to 10 men. Another lifeless and limp first 45 minutes against Mexico had the score 0–0 at halftime. In the dressing room Nicolas Anelka—known in Britain as Le Sulk because of his moody reputation—hurled a volley of foulmouthed abuse at Domenech. He was replaced by André-Pierre Gignac, not record goalscorer Thierry Henry. Demoralized and disjointed, they lost, 2–0. That's when the fun really started.

The team went on strike.

Anelka was given a chance to apologize but he declined and was sent home. The players, led by captain Patrice Evra, mutinied in protest and refused to train. To make matters worse, they did it at an open public session attended by hundreds of locals. The players had written a letter to protest the decision—incredibly it was left to Domenech to read it out to the press!

The French Football Federation released a statement with counter claims, and the day of recriminations and rows ended with the resignation of team director Jean-Louis Valentin who said he was, "sickened and disgusted." Extraordinary TV pictures showed staff and players being pulled apart before they came to blows. French president Nicolas Sarkozy ordered the country's sports minister, Roselyne Bachelot, to visit the camp and talk sense into them and her emotional lecture reportedly reduced some to tears.

Domenech changed more than half the lineup for the crucial showdown with the hosts South Africa. But Yoann Gourcuff was dismissed within 25 minutes, they lost, 2–1, and France were out, shamefully and ignominiously.

The team was made to fly home from South Africa in coach and the FFF president resigned. Domenech was replaced with Laurent Blanc, and for his first international in charge, he dropped all twenty-three players.

## CHAPTER FIVE

# THE UNLUCKY 13: THE BEST TO NEVER PLAY IN THE WORLD CUP

It's impossible to rank soccer players. Is Lionel Messi a more skillful dribbler than Diego Maradona? Has Cristiano Ronaldo more talent than Pelé?

For instance, I believe Pat Jennings was the greatest goalkeeper ever. Why? Because he was from Northern Ireland and I grew up watching him. He won trophies in England and Europe and lined up against Brazil in the World Cup on his forty-first birthday. But I never saw legendary Russian keeper Lev Yashin. Maybe he was better. How about Dino Zoff, who captained Italy to the World Cup in 1982? Or perhaps Gianluigi Buffon, who played his 1,000th match in March 2017? I've followed soccer religiously for forty years, but there was a professional league in Britain for almost a century before I first trotted up to the turnstile. My opinions are molded by those I knew in my youth and those I watch today.

Geography is important too, and a South American list of the world's greatest players will differ from one compiled in Europe. Another factor is the era the players starred in. Soccer has changed so much in the past twenty years, never mind comparing players to their predecessors from five decades ago. Today the pace is lightning fast; teams prepare for games with a GPS in their training vest, recover in cryogenic chambers, and get detailed video analysis of their opponents beamed from the other side of the planet.

So in compiling this baker's dozen of unlucky players I've been as inclusive as I can, featuring different continents, different decades, and different reasons for their exclusion. They are in no particular order—apart from the one I start with . . .

# GEORGE BEST, NORTHERN IRELAND

Fans from Ulster think he was the greatest ever. But Pelé said it as well, so it's not a belief only limited to an island in northern Europe. He was the first player to move soccer from the back page to the front page, the first playboy playmaker, the first tabloid celebrity sportsman.

Best made his debut with Manchester United at seventeen and from then on taunted and teased defenders determined to scythe down The Belfast Boy. But it was a career cut spectacularly short through illness, arrogance, and alcoholism.

He hit the headlines in 1966 in the European Cup quarterfinal against Benfica of Portugal, who had never lost at home in the competition. Best scored twice in the first 13 minutes. The local media dubbed him "O Quinto Beatle" (the fifth Beatle): the name stuck.

In 1968 they faced Benfica again in the European Cup final, and with the game tied at 1–1, Best picked up the ball, drove through the back line, and feinted past the goalkeeper before rolling it into the net. The Reds ran out 4–1 winners and Best was voted the European Footballer of the Year and Footballer of the Year in England. He was just twenty-two and this was the pinnacle of both his club and individual career: he never scaled such heights again.

Although that was the last trophy he won, in 1970 he scored six goals in an FA Cup match against Northampton, while in 1972 he chalked up 27 goals in 54 appearances and finished as the club's top-scorer for the sixth consecutive season. But the same

George Best, the Belfast Boy. One of the greatest players in history but he never made it to the World Cup with Northern Ireland.

year he announced his retirement, then came back only to regularly miss matches to spend weekends in bed with actresses and beauty queens or to party at London nightclubs. He quit again in 1973 and returned again. He made his last appearance for United on New Year's Day 1974.

He wandered the world as a soccer mercenary for a decade, fighting an increasingly alcohol-fueled self-destructive streak. He turned out for teams in South Africa, the Republic of Ireland, Australia, Scotland, Northern Ireland, and returned to Fulham in England's second tier. He had two spells in the USA, scoring 15 times in just 24 games in his first season with the Los Angeles Aztecs and being crowned the league's best midfielder in his second. He went on to appear for the Fort Lauderdale Strikers and then the San Jose Earthquakes for whom he scored the greatest goal of his career, beating more than half the Strikers team on a spellbinding run before slotting the ball past the keeper from close range.

By 1984 he was in jail, serving a three-month sentence for DUI, assaulting a police officer, and failing to answer bail. He appeared on TV shows drunk, he was divorced twice amid domestic abuse allegations, and his health deteriorated to the extent he needed a liver transplant in 2002. But it didn't stop his drinking; two years later he received another DUI, and in November 2005 he died from multiple organ failure. Hundreds of thousands of mourners lined the streets of Belfast for his funeral, and the following year the city's airport was renamed George Best Airport.

Best made his debut for Northern Ireland in 1964—six years after their appearance at the 1958 World Cup. The last of his 37 caps came in 1977—five years before their next qualification in

1982. His tragedy was to be the country's greatest-ever player slap-bang in the middle of their tournament drought.

I saw him play a handful of times. The World Cup qualifier against Holland I referenced in the Introduction was the only competitive match; the others were friendlies and testimonials. We were once on the same flight to Heathrow airport and I stood beside him at the luggage carousel. My mum claims she met him in a fish-and-chip shop in Belfast in the sixties and he asked her on a date. Apparently he was wearing a pink sweater. It's a much better story.

Bobby Tambling, the striker with the second-best goal-scoring record in Chelsea's history, told me this story. He was in charge of Cork Celtic in the League of Ireland during the 1975–76 season and they arranged for Best to fly in from England to play home games. He got a thousand pounds a match, and although it only lasted two weeks, the gate receipts for both those games totaled more than every other home game that year combined.

The Dublin club Shelbourne phoned Bobby to ask if Best would be in the team when they came to the capital. He told them no because Cork Celtic didn't get a share of the money when they played road games. So Shelbourne said if they did bring Best then they would come up with the thousand pounds! Yes, the opposition was willing to pay to have Best play against them!

Best's quotes are legendary:

"In 1969 I gave up women and alcohol. It was the worst 20 minutes of my life."
"I used to go missing a lot: Miss Canada, Miss United Kingdom, Miss World."
"I spent a lot of money on booze, birds and fast cars. The rest I just squandered."

But more telling: "They'll forget all the rubbish when I've gone and they'll remember the football."

We do George, we do. George Best, the tortured genius. The Belfast Boy.

# ALFREDO DI STÉFANO, ARGENTINA/ SPAIN

If you are involved in a kidnapping and a conspiracy theory involving a fascist dictator you can consider yourself unlucky. If you represent two different World Cup winning nations and yet still don't make the finals you probably think a higher power has it in for you. If George Best's extracurricular antics were entertaining, Alfredo Di Stéfano's off-field trials and tribulations are the stuff of a far-fetched Hollywood screenplay.

Many believe that when Real Madrid had Di Stéfano alongside Ferenc Puskás, it was the best midfield of all time. Their 7–3 win against Eintracht Frankfurt in the European Cup final in 1960 is considered the greatest game ever played. Di Stéfano notched a hat trick as Real won the Cup for the fifth straight year. He scored in every final. He was twice voted the best player in the world. He was voted Spain's greatest player of all time despite being Argentinean.

And yet he never made it onto the biggest soccer stage of all.

He signed with River Plate in Buenos Aires then moved to Millonarios of Bogotá. After sparkling displays for the Colombians on tour in Spain in 1952 both Barcelona and Real Madrid wanted to sign him. The problem was that though he was registered with Millonarios, a "piece" of him was still maintained by River Plate in Argentina, the team he had left in acrimonious circumstances after a players' strike. Barcelona negotiated with both outfits simultaneously, but when the Colombians rejected their transfer offer, they flew Di Stéfano to Spain anyway and played him in two exhibitions. But while Barca had reached a settlement with the Argentinians, Real had made a deal with the Colombians. Both clubs had agreements—but with different teams in different countries!

In a truly bizarre Solomon-like decision, the Spanish Football Federation ruled he should spend the next four years alternating between both clubs, a season at a time. Barcelona pulled out of the transfer and the animosity and rivalry from the episode still resonates through Spanish soccer today. Real fans maintain it was arrogance and sloppiness on Barca's part, while the Catalans see a dark, underhand, despicable plot reaching to the very top of the government—Real were known as The Regime Team, the favored club of dictator General Francisco Franco.

A month after making his debut, Di Stéfano scored four times in El Clasico as they crushed Barcelona, 5–0. With him as the centerpiece they dominated Europe in a way no club has before or since and Real racked up eight league championships in 10 years.

On the international stage, he scored six times in six games as Argentina won the South American championship in 1947, but Argentina refused to enter either the 1950 or 1954 World Cups. It was a fit of pique that denied one of the greatest players ever a fitting platform.

Three years after arriving in Madrid, he took citizenship—the fact he had already played for another country not much of an issue for FIFA back then—but Spain failed to qualify for the 1958 World Cup. Finally, leaving the cruelest to last, in his mid-thirties he helped his adopted nation make it to the 1962 finals in Chile.

But a muscle problem in his leg denied The Blond Arrow his final chance to grace the tournament.

In August 1963 on a preseason tour, four revolutionaries kidnapped him at gunpoint from his hotel in Caracas, Venezuela. But they wanted publicity, not money, and released him unharmed two days later. Di Stéfano spent his captivity playing dominoes, cards, and chess with the guerrillas and said the rebel commander Maximo Canales, "apologized a thousand times for the inconvenience."

Surreally, that commander changed his name and achieved worldwide fame as artist Paul del Rio. He was reunited with Di Stéfano—presumably under much more hospitable and less life-threatening circumstances—at the premiere of a film about the kidnap forty-two years after it happened. Di Stéfano died from a heart attack in July 2014 age eighty-eight and his coffin was placed on public display at the Bernabéu Stadium.

## LÁSZLÓ KUBALA, HUNGARY/ CZECHOSLOVAKIA/SPAIN

László Kubala is the greatest player you have never heard of. The only man to have played for three different nations, he failed to reach the World Cup with Hungary, Czechoslovakia, or Spain. Real Madrid and Barcelona fought for his signature. He was a refugee who fled his country in the back of a truck, and when he was banned from soccer after dodging military service, he simply started his own team. And his son falling ill saved his life.

Think Lionel Messi is Barcelona's greatest ever player? The Barcelona fans don't. They voted the Hungarian their most talented player of all time. Their official website calls the 1950s "The Kubala era." His statue stands at the stadium entrance.

He started his career as an eighteen-year-old at Ferencváros in Budapest, then moved to Czechoslovakia to avoid military service. Two years later he returned to Hungary to escape another draft. But in January 1949 with the Iron Curtain descending across Europe, he was smuggled across the border into Austria in a farm truck, and then into Italy.

He agreed to play for four-time league winners Torino in a friendly against Benfica in Lisbon, but at the last minute his son fell sick, and Kubala was worried enough to skip the trip. Torino's plane crashed on the return journey, killing everyone aboard. His child's fever saved his life.

Meanwhile, the Hungarians complained to FIFA that having fled the country, he was in breach of contract, and he was banned from international soccer for a year. As vast swathes of displaced refugees swarmed across a fragmenting Europe, his ingenious idea was to start a team full of stateless Eastern European exiles. He called it Hungaria, and as had happened with Di Stéfano, both Spanish giants fought for his signature after seeing him in exhibitions. This time Barca was victorious.

In 1951–52, his first season after the ban ended, he was on the score sheet *seven* times against Sporting de Gijón—still a record in La Liga today—as the Catalans lifted five trophies. So many fans clamored to see him that the club authorized the building of the Camp Nou, the gargantuan iconic structure that is still the biggest soccer ground in Europe. He scored 280 goals for Barca and his playing career ended as a player-coach in Canada in his forties where he played for Toronto Falcons alongside his son.

After representing both Hungary and Czechoslovakia, he adopted Spanish nationality in 1953, but just like Di Stéfano, his chance to compete at the World Cup was snatched away when he was forced to pull out injured from their 1962 squad.

At the age of sixty-five he managed 10 minutes for a Catalan XI in his own testimonial match against an International XI. He died in 2002. His great rival, but even greater friend, Di Stéfano said, "Kubala was one of the best there has ever been."

# DUNCAN EDWARDS, ENGLAND

The trio we have examined so far did not make the World Cup, but they still earned a treasure chest of personal honors and team medals. With Duncan Edwards, it's a case of what might have been. Not just a career cut short—a life cut short.

The Manchester United midfielder was renowned for his size, power, and physical presence, nicknamed "Big Dunc" and "The Tank" (and "Boom Boom" by the German press). Though critically injured in the air crash that claimed the lives of seven teammates, he fought to stay alive for two weeks, asking club staff about the kickoff time of the next game. Criminally, he was just twenty-one when he died.

United officials arrived at the teenager's house just past midnight on his birthday so he could legally sign a contract, and he became a battering ram of talent and skill around whom legendary coach Sir Matt Busby built his Busby Babes. He made his debut aged just sixteen years and 185 days, the youngest player ever in England's top tier. Imagine a tenth grader turning out for an American professional sports team today.

He earned his first international cap aged a grandfatherly eighteen, and it would be another forty-three years before England picked a younger player. But he was not exempt from national service, and won the league while serving in the army! He was released weekly to play for the Red Devils, though in return he had to turn out for the army team as well.

In February 1958, United traveled to Yugoslavia to play Red Star Belgrade in the second leg of the European Cup quarterfinal. The 3–3 tie was enough to see them advance to the semifinal, and their chartered plane touched down to refuel in a slow-blanketed Munich.

In one of those "sliding doors" moments, the plane had been delayed an hour because winger Johnny Berry lost his passport. Would things have been different if they had touched down in Germany sixty minutes earlier? The weather was atrocious and treacherous, a canopy of low cloud and snow covering the airport.

The pilot tried to take off twice and abandoned both attempts. The passengers returned to the terminal. Edwards sent a telegram to his landlady reading that the flight had been canceled and they would be home the next day. Then the pilot decided to try again.

But there was too much slush for the wheels to get the traction and speed the plane needed to climb. The aircraft skidded off the end of the runway, crashing into a house and a hut containing a truck full of fuel and tires. It ignited in a deadly fireball.

Seven players and sixteen other passengers out of the forty-four aboard lost their lives. Edwards survived the initial impact but internal bleeding and complications from an artificial kidney beat him and he died in hospital on February 21, 1958.

United assistant coach Jimmy Murphy said: "When I used to hear Muhammad Ali proclaim to the world that he was the greatest, I would always smile. The greatest of them all was a footballer named Duncan Edwards."

# RYAN GIGGS, WALES

From a Manchester United star whose career was guillotined to one who's lasted longer than some democracies. Ryan Giggs spent more than 20 years at the pinnacle of the world game. All with the same club.

He collected thirteen Premier League titles, four FA Cups, three League Cups, and two European Champions League cups. All with the same club.

He played almost 1,000 matches. All with the same club.

He holds the record for most assists in the Premier League (162). He is the only player to have played in twenty-two successive Premier League seasons, and scored in twenty-one successive Premier League seasons. All with the same club.

He is the only player to have scored in seventeen different Champions League tournaments and the oldest scorer in the competition's history. All with the same club.

Like his fellow tricky winger Best, he too is from a small British nation that never qualified for the World Cup. But he did manage a smidgen of international tournament experience, captaining Great Britain when London hosted the Olympics.

United coach Alex Ferguson turned up at the family home and persuaded Giggs to sign for them on his fourteenth birthday, snatching him away from their crosstown rivals City. In his first full campaign he was voted Young Player of the Year, in his second season he won the league title, in his third year United claimed the league and cup double. By the turn of the millennium, United had lifted the championship six times in eight years.

Sometimes one moment defines a player's career. The Cruyff turn against Sweden, Tardelli's goal celebration against West

Germany, Maradona's second strike against England. Giggs's came in the FA Cup semifinal replay against Arsenal in 1999.

Picking the ball up in his own half he goes on a weaving run, turning inside and out as he leaves the whole Arsenal defense for dead before burying the ball into the net off the crossbar. Ecstatic, he whips off his shirt and takes off running at full speed, chased by his teammates and delirious fans. In 2013, he made his 1,000th competitive appearance (he put his longevity down to yoga), and in May 2014 he retired at forty on the same day he was installed as assistant coach at Old Trafford.

On the international stage, Giggs plowed the same furrow as Best, a genius supported by lesser lights, though he was frequently absent from non-competitive matches, once going on a streak of missing eighteen consecutive friendlies. He quit Wales a full seven years before he stopped playing for United, though in 2012 he broke yet another record when he became the oldest goalscorer in the Olympics a few months shy of his 39th birthday.

## ERIC CANTONA, FRANCE

We finish our Manchester United quartet with their most controversial player ever. If the defining image of Giggs was his shirt-waving sprint after his wonder solo goal, the iconic picture of Eric Cantona is him flying into the stands to aim a kung fu kick at a fan.

I remember the night in January 1995 that King Eric (as United supporters called him) launched himself into the crowd at Crystal Palace. I heard about it on the radio and called my friend Michael from California who was working in London. I told him to watch the soccer highlights show that evening as it would be extraordinary, and when the program opened, the host, with no introduction or preamble, said something like, "Tonight we are going to show you something that has never before in history been witnessed at an English football ground." It was that big a deal.

Cantona had been sent off for kicking an opponent, and as he walked back to the locker room he took exception to an abusive fan, so he jumped the advertising boards and planted his feet into the fan's chest. I recall the outraged supporter's sense of victimization as his claimed he tossed a mild invective along the lines of, "It's an early bath for you Cantona!" as if he had attended the match straight from a Victorian tea party.

It subsequently emerged he had run down eleven rows of stairs to scream, "Fuck off back to France, you French motherfucker." So, a little bit different then.

Cantona came ever so tantalizingly close to playing in the World Cup. One mishit cross . . . that's all that denied him his global showcase. A passage of play that ripped French soccer apart.

Les Blues, a top seed in qualifying, needed only one tie from their last two home games to make the 1994 tournament. They were 2–1 ahead to Israel, the lowest-ranked country, but in a calamitous final seven minutes they contrived to concede twice and snatch defeat from the jaws of victory.

Still, they just had to tie against Bulgaria, and once Cantona volleyed them in front they were back on track. However, the Eastern Europeans equalized. In the last minute France won a free kick by the corner flag. But instead of taking the ball to the corner and running down the clock, substitute David Ginola crossed the ball towards Cantona. With 18 seconds left! The pass was over-hit and recovered by the Bulgarians, it fell to striker Emil Kostadinov and he lashed it into the net. France were out.

Coach Gerard Houllier called Ginola "the murderer" of French hopes, adding, "He sent an Exocet missile through the heart of French football and committed a crime against the team." Those fateful few seconds also murdered Cantona's chance of World Cup glory. When the next tournament came along he had retired from soccer. France won it.

Cantona's near-feral behavior began with Auxerre when he was fined for punching a teammate in the face, then he was suspended for two months after an unhinged martial arts-style tackle on an opponent. He was sold to Marseille for a record transfer fee but they banned him for a month after he ripped off his shirt when he was substituted. He had already been indefinitely exiled from the national team after calling coach Henri Michel "a bag of shit" in a TV interview.

He was loaned to Montpellier and banned for ten days after throwing his boots into a teammate's face. He was traded to Nîmes and summoned to a disciplinary hearing by the French Football Federation after throwing the ball at a referee. His one-month suspension was doubled when he approached each member of the panel individually and called them all idiots.

He signed for Leeds in England and they won the league title and the following year he was transferred to Manchester United: Cantona, his collar turned up, his chest thrust out, exuding arrogance and Gallic swagger, was the first player to win consecutive titles with different clubs. He was fined for spitting at a fan on his return to Leeds, and although United retained the championship the following year, he was banned for five games after being red-carded in successive matches.

After his kung fu attack, Cantona admitted a criminal charge of assault and was sentenced to community service. He was banned from soccer worldwide for eight months and stripped off the French national team captaincy. He never played for his country again. He returned to the United lineup the following season and went on to win six league titles in seven years before hanging up his boots.

In 2011 he was employed by the New York Cosmos as their Director of Soccer. He was fired three years later for punching a photographer. Never change, Eric.

# GEORGE WEAH, LIBERIA

I was at Wembley Stadium in 2000 when George Weah led the line for Chelsea in their 1–0 win against Aston Villa in the FA Cup final. At thirty-three, he played all but the last two minutes on the expansive, energy-sapping field on a hot day in late May.

What I remember best about him that day is something I can still picture in my mind's eye. Seconds before kickoff he stood motionless, his head tilted back and his arms outstretched, praying. In contrast to the tortured demons that guided Cantona, Weah was the closest thing the impoverished country of Liberia have had to a benevolent angel.

He played for the team. He coached the team. He funded the team, personally paying their travel expenses. And when his playing days were over, he ran for political office. His dedication and devotion to his country is astonishing in the days of spoiled and self-centered sporting superstars.

Just surviving is a Herculean task in the west African nation where almost nine in every ten citizens live below the poverty line. That Weah escaped to become the only African named FIFA World Player of the Year is nothing short of miraculous.

In 1988, he joined Monaco and was then transferred to Paris Saint-Germain where he won a trophy every season for the next three years. In his physical prime and the form of his life, he signed for Italian giants AC Milan.

If you want to know why soccer fans of my generation revere him, search on the Internet for his goal against Verona in September 1996. It's one of the greatest individual strikes you will ever see.

Milan are defending a corner and Weah is six yards from his own goal-line. The corner is hit long and he instantly controls the ball, setting off straight down the middle of the field. He leaves opponents in his wake, his strength and acceleration taking him past bodies as they fly in to stop him. Thirteen seconds after receiving the ball at one end he scores in the other end without a single other player touching it.

He won two league titles with Milan, was voted World Player of the Year in 1995, and was named African Player of the Century. Not bad for a bare-footed boy who learned to kick a ball in the trash-strewn slums of Monrovia.

He played for Liberia for 16 years, almost making the 2002 World Cup with a squad featuring players from clubs in nine countries on four different continents. His consolation was to twice represent his country at the 1996 and 2002 African Cup of Nations.

After his retirement, he ran for various political offices in Liberia and won the 2017 presidential election. It's for this off-field dedication to his country that he is known as King George, and not because he slalomed his way through the best defenses in Europe.

# JARI LITMANEN, FINLAND

From Monrovia in Liberia, the wettest capital city on earth, to the frozen landscape of northern Europe and Finland, the home of the Lapps. Jari Litmanen's international career spanned an amazing four decades.

I went to Finland in May 1984 to see Northern Ireland play a World Cup qualifier while we were enjoying a purple patch in our history. The Finns were the bottom seeds in the group. Of course, we lost, 1–0.

The occasional good result is the height of Finland's international ambitions. But Litmanen, an outrageously talented midfielder, was committed. After making his debut in October 1989 he racked up a total of 137 caps and scored 32 times, no mean feat playing for such a small nation. When he hit the back of the net on his farewell appearance in November 2010 he became the oldest player to score a goal in the European Championship qualifiers. In Finland, he is simply known as Kuningas—The King.

He will forever be associated with the Ajax team of the 1990s, considered one of the greatest squads ever assembled. Both his parents were soccer internationals, and he played for three clubs in Finland before going to Amsterdam in 1992. In his second season, he was voted Player of the Year as Ajax dominated the Dutch division, going undefeated in 52 games on their way to three successive league titles.

It was the club's European performances that belied the accusation they were a big fish in an uncompetitive small pond. They won the 1995 European Champions League after beating AC Milan, who were appearing in their third straight final.

Along with the Nigerian Finidi George, Litmanen was the only other starting foreigner, and he became the first Finn to lift the trophy. They were unbeaten in the competition for a record 19 matches.

They lost the final the following year to Juventus in a penalty shootout after a 1–1 tie. I watched it in a hotel in St. Petersburg, Florida, and was transfixed by their skill and precision. They should have won. Litmanen was the tournament's top scorer that year and remains the club's highest European goalscorer.

As the rich European clubs circled like vultures and then descended upon the Dutch carrion, Litmanen was poached by Barcelona. In 2000 he turned out 32 times for the Catalans, but despite playing another 11 years he never again managed as many matches in a season. His ankle was so frequently hurt he was nicknamed "Glass Man."

He transferred to Liverpool but the year they won a trio of domestic and European trophies he missed all three finals through injury. Like a despondent medieval minstrel, he wandered Europe but neither found his voice nor an audience to listen to his song.

He returned to Ajax, moved back to Finland, went to Germany, signed for Malmo in Sweden (where he made just 10 league appearances in three years), joined Fulham in England but left without playing a match, and finally ended up back in his homeland.

It was a painful odyssey, but in 2011, age forty and in his final year as a professional, he scored as HJK Helsinki won the Finnish Cup final to go with their third championship in a row. He finished as a Double winner after playing 18 league games, the most in a decade. He signed off with the hottest of Indian summers in the coldest of climates.

# BERND SCHUSTER, WEST GERMANY

These days, fathers attend the birth of their children. If a dad missed his child coming into the world he would be ridiculed and derided for being uncaring and heartless. But Bernd Schuster probably never played in the World Cup because he thought that being at the birth of his son was more important than playing a game in Albania.

Schuster, a maverick and a hothead, was only the fourth player since World War II to transfer from Barcelona to their hated rivals Real Madrid; when he became persona non grata there he moved to their despised crosstown enemies, Atlético.

I saw the striker in November 1982 in Belfast for West Germany. Northern Ireland beat them, 1–0, a fantastic win against the reigning European champions who had been World Cup runners-up that summer. No heavenly joy that night for the Blond Angel, an ironic moniker as many colleagues and coaches would have named him after the occupants of the other place in the afterlife.

He spent two years with Cologne before being snapped up by Barcelona in 1980, the same year he won the European Championship with the Germans and was voted into the Team of the Tournament.

But he missed the 1982 World Cup thanks to a horrific tackle by Atlético Bilbao's defender Andoni Goikoetxea that broke his knee and almost ended his career. Known by the charming nickname "The Butcher of Bilbao," Goikoetxea repeated his party trick on Maradona a few years later. By 1984, Schuster had retired from international soccer at just twenty-four years old.

He refused a call up for a match in Tirana to be with his wife for the birth of their second son. It was interpreted as a snub to his country, and shortly afterwards, fed up battling both the authorities and coach Jupp Derwall, he quit the team. He won 21 caps for West Germany and had been on the losing side just twice—to Brazil and Northern Ireland.

At Barca, he clung on for eight years despite a revolving door of coaches (three, starting with László Kubala, in his first year alone), and regular disputes over tactics, money, and teammates. In 1985, they won the league and the following year reached the final of the European Cup, losing on penalties to Steaua Bucharest of Romania. With five minutes left Schuster was substituted and stormed out of the stadium in a rage. The club had a scapegoat, and at the height of his career he did not play a single match the following season, left to rot in the reserves as punishment.

After nearly 300 appearances, he gave the club and their fans the proverbial middle finger and headed to Real Madrid. Rubbing a particularly spicy salt into their Spanish sausage, he inspired Los Blancos to back-to-back league championships. Then when you thought the rambunctious Teutonic had settled down, he rocked up at Atlético, twice winning the Spanish cup and becoming the first player to win that trophy with three different teams.

At thirty-three, he returned to Germany for three years with Bayer Leverkusen. In his second year, he achieved the unprecedented clean sweep of coming first, second, and third in the Goal of the Season award. The winning strike, a rocket from the halfway line, was also named Goal of the Decade.

# ARSENIO ERICO, PARAGUAY

We have eight Europeans and an African, so let's turn to the player generally accepted as the greatest South American to never make it: Arsenio Erico from Paraguay.

He didn't walk out on the team, he didn't lose out through injury, he didn't play for a small nation who never qualified. His international career was in a twenty-year period in which his country didn't enter the World Cup—hell, he never even played an official FIFA international match! Paraguay ignored the 1938 World Cup, then after the withdrawal of Ecuador and Peru in 1950 they qualified automatically for the next one without playing a match. But it was three years too late for Erico.

In an age when it was commonplace to switch countries (as we have seen), Erico endeared himself to the Paraguayans for rejecting a king's ransom from Argentina to accept nationalization. His principled stance was the soccer world's loss.

He was born more than a century ago but is still the highest scorer the Argentinean league has ever seen—chalking up all 295 goals with one club. No less a light than Alfredo Di Stéfano thought he may have been the best player ever.

He was just fifteen when he made his debut for Club Nacional in Asunción, and though World War II denied him a chance to play at the World Cup, it was the Chaco War that gave him his career. The Red Cross arranged exhibitions to raise money for victims, and after a pulsating performance in Argentina, Independiente signed him in May 1934.

His goals won them the Primera División three times. He scored many with his head, his elevation and ability in the air earning him the nickname "The Red Jumper" after the color of the team's shirts. The Argentineans begged him to join the national team for the 1938 World Cup in France, but despite a huge financial offer he refused to turn his back on his homeland.

But he did claim another cash reward—by deliberately missing the goal.

In 1938 a cigarette company offered a large sum to anyone who scored 43 goals that season to publicize their new Cigarillos 43 brand. Erico hit the target with two matches left, but was informed the offer only stood if he finished the year with that exact number of strikes. The club had already won the league, so in the final games he missed easy chances and passed when better placed to shoot. Decades later, he admitted he had done it to win the money.

He died in 1977 and was buried in Buenos Aires, but thirty-three years later his body was repatriated to Paraguay, his coffin draped in both flags of the countries he loved. In these days of corporate sponsorship and branding, seventy years after he played for them, Nacional's stadium still bears his name.

# ABEDI AYEW, GHANA

You may not recognize the name. This African superstar is better known as Abedi Pele.

The Ghanaian hero is an icon across the continent for his trailblazer status in soccer's upper echelons. But when he was given his nickname as a kid in Accra, he didn't even know who the Brazilian was. He never made the tournament, but the talent packed into his genes led to *three* of his sons representing the Black Stars at World Cups.

Usually players go to the Middle East at the end of their careers looking for a final payday before retirement, but bizarrely Pele started in Qatar at seventeen after playing in his country's African Cup of Nations win in 1982.

He bounced from there to Switzerland to Benin and back to Ghana, but it was with his transfer to Marseille in France at twenty-three that his career took off. For three years, he was at the heart of the greatest period in the club's history, voted African Footballer of the Year each of those years and named Player of the Tournament at the 1992 African Nations Cup.

He never scored many goals, 12 was his best return in 1993 as the team from the Riviera won their second successive title (incidentally, a Ghanaian team he later coached won 31–0 in a promotion playoff, their rivals won 28–0. The 31 goals in 90 minutes was just one less than he scored in his last five years in Europe added together!). With Pele it was quality, not quantity. His strikes were invariably spectacular, either waltzing his way through a packed defense as if it didn't exist, or hammering a precision shot into the top corner from 30 yards.

In 1991, Marseille won the league and lost the European Cup final on penalties, the following year they won the league again, in 1993 they finally won the European Cup (now renamed the European Champions League) after defeating AC Milan, 1–0. They remain the only French club to ever lift the prestigious trophy. Pele's dynamic, nonstop performance in a cluttered midfield won him the Man of the Match award. It was his swan song in the white shirt and he was transferred to Lyon, seeing out his playing days in Italy and Germany before quitting at thirty-five after another turn in the Middle East.

Ghana didn't make their first finals appearance until 2006 with a crop of stars who grew up inspired by their countryman's exploits as he rampaged and raked his way through the cream of European talent. But three of his four sons were on the World Cup rosters for Ghana in 2010 and 2014. That surely, is the next best thing to making it yourself.

# VALENTINO MAZZOLA, ITALY

Valentino Mazzola won just 12 international caps. His playing days were shredded by war, then curtailed by tragedy. But fans still revere the man who was the fulcrum for one of the most famous teams in the rich history of Italian soccer, the all-conquering "Grande Torino" club of the 1940s who won five successive league titles.

He was unlucky to play in the most tumultuous decade of the twentieth century. And in a slower-paced age when players regularly prolonged their time on the field into their late thirties and even forties, he died alongside his teammates in the plane crash that wiped out the squad.

The Turin outfit regularly provided *nine* of the Italian national team players. In May 1947 against Hungary they went one better—every single outfield player was from Torino. How did the Torino goalkeeper feel when that starting 11 was announced?

When he was nineteen, Mazzola turned down AC Milan to sign for the works team of Alfa Romeo as that offer included a mechanic apprenticeship in their factory. When darkness descended across Europe in 1939 he was called into the navy and stationed in Venice. He starred for the navy team as a forward and was snapped up by the local club Venezia, the story goes after impressing in a tryout in which he played barefoot because he didn't want to risk damaging his cleats.

In 1942, he made his debut for the national team and was sold to Torino, the club finding him a "job" as an essential wartime worker at Turin's Fiat factory to escape military service. They won a truncated league in 1943, were crowned champions again in 1946 when full-scale soccer resumed, and swept the next three titles as well, each season with an increasing number of record points. They were unbeaten at home for six years.

The most remarkable thing about this all-conquering club is that they were coached by the Hungarian Jew Ernest Erbstein. He had lived in Italy until 1938 when Mussolini's increasingly strident anti-Semitic rhetoric forced him to flee back home. Although deported to a concentration camp he had survived and returned to the club after the armistice.

They were crowned champions in 1949 but never saw out the season. Coming back from a friendly in Lisbon against Benfica their plane smashed into a hill outside Turin in heavy rain, strong crosswinds, and low clouds. All the players, staff, and journalists aboard died.

Like Manchester United at Munich, the Superga air disaster decimated not just the playing staff but the club's heart and soul. Unlike United though, who won the European Cup within a decade, Torino never recovered. In the nearly seventy years since they have won a solitary league title. Both Mazzola's sons became Seria A players.

He was famous for rolling up his sleeves as a message both to his teammates and the crowd that it was time to dig in. It was a tragedy that his fight was extinguished at such a young age.

# JOÃO DOMINGOS PINTO, PORTUGAL

We end with the cruelest way of all to miss out. To play every game in World Cup qualifying. To be named in the squad. To fly to the World Cup. And then to not play a minute because you are struck down with a disease that sounds like it belongs to sailors in the fourteenth century.

João Domingos Pinto (his middle name is used to avoid confusion with his namesake who did play in the 2002 World Cup) was Portugal's greatest right back.

He broke into the Porto team as a teenager and played for the next 17 years. He collected an astonishing array of league medals as Porto bulldozed through the Primeira Liga: Between 1985 and 1997 they lifted the title nine times, a blinding, pulverizing spell of success. Pinto won 25 cups in his 407 appearances.

But Porto weren't just flat-track bullies. They defeated German powerhouse Bayern Munich in the 1987 European Cup, and then went to Tokyo and beat Peñarol of Uruguay to lift the Intercontinental Cup. They were officially and unequivocally the best club in the world.

Pinto made his international bow in 1983 and won 70 caps for Portugal in 13 years. I saw him in Belfast in a European Championship qualifier in 1994 (we lost of course). He was ever-present in their successful campaign to qualify for the 1986 World Cup in Mexico, but he was struck down with pleurisy days before it started and did not recover in time to step on the field. By the time they next made it to the tournament he had retired.

But that Portugal appearance in 1986, their first at the finals in twenty years, is seen as an embarrassment even today. They lost defender António Veloso before it started when he tested positive for steroids. Their training base was in a laughably awful condition, the players went on strike over a dispute about bonuses, and when they did practice they turned their shirts inside out to hide the name of the team's sponsors. Portugal beat England in their opening match but then contrived to lose to both Poland and Morocco and were eliminated in the first round.

So maybe, just maybe, it's sometimes lucky to miss out on the World Cup . . .

# CHAPTER SIX

# A PERFECT TEN

The ten "best" games in World Cup history depends on the subjective prism through which you view them.

As a Northern Ireland fan, I could write about the 1958 match when we held the world champions West Germany to a tie, or the contest in 1982 when we beat the host nation Spain. As an American supporter, I could highlight the USA's 1950 victory over England (I did, elsewhere in this book).

Even as a neutral, your view is influenced by where and with whom you watch. A tourist in a jammed bar in Buenos Aires when Argentina beat Holland to lift the trophy for the first time in 1978 would have a diametrically opposed memory of the same final than a traveler who was in an Amsterdam pub.

Nationality and geography cloud your judgment, as does recency bias (a stock market term meaning more weight is placed on recent events which are then overemphasized compared to older memories). Today's matches are recorded with high-definition, slow-mo cameras capturing the trickery and wizardry from dozens of different angles. How can you compare these with the grainy, stuttering black-and-white images from games decades before the digital age?

I've followed half of the twenty tournaments, and since 1986 I've missed just a handful of contests. The second-round game at that tournament in Mexico that ended Belgium 4, Soviet Union 3, is one of my favorites. I was a pimply sixteen-year-old watching it in my living room in Belfast, but I remember the excitement as goals were traded like basketball points and I was lost in a late-night undiluted thrill of the sporting spectacle even though I had no dog in the fight.

I could go on and on about what I might have done, so here is what I *did* do. I picked ten matches, half I watched, half I read about, from every decade of World Cup history. Scintillating per-formances, impressive displays, major upsets—or just damn fine soccer matches:

## 1938, First Round
### Brazil 6, Poland 5

The jumpy footage on YouTube contains a couple of minutes of action from the first hour, as if the cameraman had to run home for dinner or just got bored and stopped recording. For me there are two noteworthy moments from the clash in Strasbourg.

The first is the tackle that gives away the penalty leading to Poland's first goal. When striker Ernest Wilimowski gets past the defender, the Brazilian simply grabs him by the waist and hauls him to the ground. I'm not sure it would even have been legal in rugby.

Secondly, the subsequent spot-kick is the slowest, most casu-ally-struck penalty I have ever seen. The taker is not so much laid-back as comatose when he waltzes up, and the ball takes an age to finally trickle in.

Poland (with goalkeeper Walter Brom at seventeen still the youngest keeper ever to appear on a finals' roster, though because of World War II it was a decade before he made his debut) were backed by thousands of emigrant Polish fans, mostly coal miners, while the locals were keen to see the exotic South Americans.

Brazil were heavy favorites, and their outstanding player Leônidas da Silva, nicknamed "The Black Diamond," opened the scoring in the 18th minute. Five minutes later Fryderyk Scherfke equalized with his leisurely penalty, but goals from Romeu and José Perácio gave the South Americans a comfortable 3–1 lead at the break.

In the second half, the rain came. The heavy conditions now favored the Poles, and Wilimowski hit the target twice within six minutes to tie it up after an hour. Then the downpour stopped. Perácio's second put Brazil 4–3 ahead, but with almost the last kick Wilimowski completed an outstanding hat trick to force extra time.

Leônidas had thrown away his cleats because he thought he could play better without them in the mud, but the Swedish referee had made him put them back on. His boot got stuck in the quicksand-like field and came off, but he still scored to make it 5–4. A minute before the end of the first half, his boot back on, he completed a hat trick too.

But the dogged Poles refused to die, and with two minutes to go Wilimowski scored his *fourth* to claw it back to 6–5. With seconds left Erwin Nyc hit the bar—but they couldn't level it up. This end-to-end goal-fest began the World Cup love affair that global soccer fans now have with the Boys from Brazil.

# 1950, Final Game
## Uruguay 2, Brazil 1

If the 1938 contest was when the soccer world's love affair with the Samba Boys was born, the next tournament was when Brazil's relationship with the sport almost died. The 1950 final was a cataclysmic shock that reverberated through the national psyche and impacted the nation for years. Isolated from the ravages of two world wars, it's the event used to divide the country into "before" and "after."

It's listed by FIFA as the final, but with the last four teams in a round-robin group it turned out that way by accident rather than design. However, it's a misnomer to call it a winner-take-all showdown as the hosts merely needed a tie to be crowned champions.

The largest, most-expectant soccer crowd in history, estimated at 200,000 spectators, crammed into the Maracanã Stadium in Rio for the formality of the match against Uruguay, and the newspaper *O Mundo* printed an early edition proclaiming the Seleção the world champions.

At halftime, the match was scoreless, but fewer than 80 seconds after the restart Friaça's header put the hosts ahead, and the Brazilian Football Confederation's advance commissioning of twenty-two gold medals seemed justified.

Enter Uruguayan captain Obdulio Varela. To insulate his team from the emotion emanating from the mammoth triple-tiered cathedral he grabbed the ball, clung onto it, and harangued the referee, claiming the strike was offside. He delayed the restart, calmed his teammates, and by the time they kicked off the ecstatic fans had quietened.

The Uruguayans became the biggest party-poopers in history. Juan Schiaffino equalized, then with 11 minutes to go Alcides Ghiggia burst into the penalty area and his shot beat goalkeeper Moacir Barbosa at his near post.

On a chaotic field afterwards, the trophy was presented to the Uruguayan captain almost as an afterthought in the midst of a jostling crowd whip-sawing between anger and confusion. Pelé said it was the first time he saw his father cry.

Barbosa was blamed for the defeat and never forgiven, later working as a cleaner at the Maracanã and burning the goalposts in an attempt at exorcism. In 1993, forty-three years later, he was turned away from a Brazilian training camp by a superstitious squad fearful his bad luck would rub off on them.

The stupendous, tremendous upset left two legacies. The match is known as the Maracanazo, "The Maracanã Blow," a term still used in South America to describe an underdog victory. Also, the public and press blamed the team's "unpatriotic" white shirts and believed the tragedy had permanently cursed them. By the next tournament Brazil wore yellow shirts and blue shorts.

**1954, First Round**
**Hungary 8, West Germany 3**
**Final**
**West Germany 3, Hungary 2**

If the form book was tossed out the window in 1950, four years later it was hurled through the glass, tied to a rocket, and fired into orbit. Never in the twenty finals has there been a heavier favorite than Hungary. It's known as "The Miracle of Bern," back in pre-hyperbolic days when a miracle was something miraculous and not a social media posting when you snagged a parking spot close to the cinema.

For West Germany, it was the defining moment that put the new nation on the path to becoming the confident power that dominated Europe. In contrast, some historians believe the defeat contributed to the unhappiness that helped spark the Hungarian Revolution of 1956.

It was David vs. Goliath—if David had been forced to fight blindfolded with one arm tied behind his back. And Goliath had been given a machine gun.

The Hungarians were Olympic champions nicknamed The Mighty Magyars. They had not lost in more than four years, still an international record, and entered the tournament unbeaten in 31 matches. They were the Golden Team led by Ferenc Puskás, "the Galloping Major." Between 1950 and 1956, when the revolution broke the side up, they played 50 matches, winning 42 and tying seven. The one they lost was the one that mattered most. Against a team that had not even existed four years previously.

The German kick that probably won the World Cup was not the winning goal in the final. It came two weeks previously in their first-round match when towering defender Werner Liebrich's crunching tackle on Puskás left him with a fractured ankle. Hungary won that match, 8–3, but the Germans had played their reserve side, gambling they would beat Turkey in a playoff and advance to the knockout stage. They did, strolling through, 7–2.

Puskás missed the quarterfinal and semifinal but it had hardly hampered the Hungarians, who racked up a ridiculous 25 goals in four games. Still injured, he was rushed back for the final and pounced to open the scoring in the sixth minute. Around 100 seconds later, Zoltán Czibor doubled the lead. It was going to be a rout. The Hungarian government's advance printing of celebratory postage stamps was vindicated (Have we been here before?).

Incredibly, 10 minutes later the match was tied as Max Morlock poked home a deflected cross and Helmut Rahn turned in a corner kick. The Hungarians laid siege but the winner wouldn't come—twice they hit the woodwork, twice the ball was scrambled off the goal line.

Instead, with six minutes left the unthinkable happened and Rahn scored his second. Puskás, strapped up and gritting through the pain, thought he had equalized at the end but it was ruled offside.

The final was the first time since the war the German national anthem was played at a major sporting event. "Suddenly Germany was somebody again," said Franz Beckenbauer.

Hungary continued to dominate after the tournament, playing a further 19 games, winning 16, and tying three. But it was no consolation. They had fluffed their lines when it mattered.

## 1966, First Round
### North Korea 1, Italy 0

The Italians were neither the first nor the last powerhouse to be embarrassed at the World Cup by a rank outsider. But with this victory, the North Koreans became the first country from outside the Americas or Europe to get beyond the first round. It would be another two decades before it happened again.

The 1966 tournament marked a turning point for FIFA and its bias towards the strongholds of Europe and South America. Africa, Asia, and Oceania were awarded just a single place between them, so when the Africans boycotted the competition in protest, the Koreans represented all three regions after negotiating a two-legged playoff against Australia.

The nation is mysterious and secretive today, so imagine how much more of a curiosity their players were more than half a century ago. They were shuffled off to play at Ayresome Park in Middlesbrough, a chemical-refining center in the economically disadvantaged northeast of England.

Tense diplomatic relations between the isolationist regime and the West meant that the UK refused to even recognize the country, and pregame ceremonies were curtailed so their national anthem would not be heard. A stamp design incorporating the flags of the nations at the finals was vetoed by the British government who refused to have their flag on UK mail.

Italy, double World Cup winners, only needed a tie to progress against their nimble, diminutive opponents, described in one newspaper as, "whimsical Orientals." The Koreans attacked from the kickoff, and after half an hour Italian captain Giacomo Bulgarelli aggravated a knee injury in a sliding tackle. He hobbled off, and with no substitutes allowed, the Azzurri played for an hour a man down. Three minutes before halftime the ball was headed into the Italian penalty area, it bounced once, and Pak Doo-ik slammed it into the net.

After the break the Italians rained shots down on the Korean goal, but all either missed the target or were saved by goalkeeper Lee Chang Myung. What the *Daily Express* called, "a country known only for war" had made the World Cup quarterfinal.

Ayresome Park was demolished thirty years later and is now a housing development called The Turnstile. But in its midst is a bronze cast of a cleat imprint sitting on the exact spot where Pak

Doo-ik struck the shot that is still remembered by the people of Middlesbrough today.

## 1970, Semifinal
### Italy 4, West Germany 3

A friend from New Orleans spent her birthday in 2017 at the World Cup qualifier between Mexico and the USA at the Azteca Stadium. I told her it was important she tracked down a plaque to a game played there forty-seven years earlier.

That gladiatorial slugfest between two championship fighters is known as "The Match of the Century." The hosts erected a monument commemorating it at the entrance to the iconic venue that pays homage to a titanic struggle, a see-sawing spectacle that ebbed and flowed for two hours. It's the only World Cup game with five goals in extra time—in fact, six in 20 minutes—and it's all the more surprising because for the first 89 minutes they had only managed one between them.

Italy went 1–0 ahead early on through Roberto Boninsegna's precise strike, but the stifling heat, breath-halting altitude, and grandeur of the occasion strangled the creativity out of the fight. Midway through the second half, Franz Beckenbauer was cynically chopped down as he accelerated towards goal. He dislocated his shoulder, but as the two permitted replacements had already been used he continued wearing a sling rather than leave his team with ten men.

The Germans pressed but the resolute Italians held out, retreating deeper and deeper. However, if the World Cup has taught us anything it is never write off the Germans: with the last kick of the match, in the third minute of injury time, defender

Karl-Heinz Schnellinger volleyed home to force another 30 minutes.

Gerd Muller put the Germans ahead but the lead only lasted four minutes until Tarcisio Burgnich brought it back to 2–2. A minute before halftime in extra time, at a psychologically crucial point, Luigi Riva powered in a shot to regain the lead for the Italians—and the pendulum swung back in their favor.

Still, Die Mannschaft came back. Muller leveled it yet again with a diving close-range header, but just 20 *seconds* after the restart, Italy swept back in front when Gianni Rivera converted an angled cross. This time they were able to seal the deal, winning the breathtaking battle, 4–3.

My friend never found the plaque, by the way.

# 1982, Semifinal
### France 3, West Germany 3 (West Germany win 5–4 on penalties)

It's crazy to think that if West Germany had tied up the game at 4–4 in that 1970 semifinal the winner would have been decided by a coin toss. A dozen years later, for the first time, penalty kicks determined the victor.

This is a game remembered because of an ugly, unpunished challenge that overshadowed the quality on show, the flair and inventiveness of the French against the iron will and resolute mentality of the Germans.

It should have been a battle between two of the greatest players of their generation: the reigning European Footballer of the Year in Karl-Heinz Rummenigge lining up against Michel Platini, who would be crowned World Player of the Year in both 1984 and 1985. But the German was struggling with a hamstring injury and started on the bench.

Pierre Littbarski's first-time shot put the Germans ahead, 10 minutes later Platini, kissing the ball before placing it on the spot, equalized from a penalty.

Approaching the hour mark, controversy. French substitute Patrick Battiston had only been on the field a few minutes and chased a defense-splitting pass from Platini. German goalkeeper Harald Schumacher raced out of his box and as the Frenchman hit the ball, Schumacher turned his body and his hip smacked into Battiston's face. The ball trickled wide as Battiston lay crumpled and unconscious. He had his vertebrae broken, lost two teeth, and later slipped into a coma as medical staff gave him oxygen. Platini said he thought he was dead. Unruffled, Schumacher ran through stretching exercises and did not bother to check on him. The referee never even awarded a foul and play resumed with a goal kick.

If you watch the slow-motion replay from the camera behind the goal, look at the Dutch referee. He is tracking the ball and not the two players so he never sees the collision. Battiston recovered and went on to win the European Championship with France two years later.

It was 1–1 after 90 minutes, but in extra time Les Blues found their second wind, the loss of their defender inspiring rather than demoralizing them. Marius Tresor put them ahead and Alain Giresse made it 3–1.

Enter Rummenigge the substitute. He popped up to poke home from close range, then Klaus Fischer leveled it with an acrobatic overhead bicycle kick. The final 10 minutes dawdled at walking pace, both teams exhausted like two past-their-prime heavyweight boxers clinging to one another and praying for the bell.

So, as it edged towards midnight in Seville, penalty kicks, the French to go first. The first five were all converted, 3–2 to France. But Uli Stielike's attempt was saved by Jean-Luc Ettori and he collapsed to the floor in anguish. Then Schumacher stopped Didier Six's shot. The keeper picked up the ball, oozing arrogance, and taunted his opposite number. Littbarski scored, 3–3. Platini and Rummenigge made it 4–4. Now it was sudden death.

But we knew how it would end and who was destined to be the hero. Schumacher saved from Maxime Bossis and Horst Hrubesch won it for the Germans. French coach Michel Hidalgo said, "They were all crying like children in the dressing room. We had to force them to undress and get into the showers." The French nation, in a newspaper poll, voted Schumacher the least popular person in history—ahead of Adolf Hitler.

Platini called this "my most beautiful game." But for the non-German soccer world, it had an ugly ending.

## 1990, First Round
### Cameroon 1, Argentina 0

The curtain raiser is always exciting. I don't mean the bloated opening ceremony, flag-waving children, singers and dancers, Diana Ross missing a shot from eight inches . . . I mean the soccer. After years of qualification and months of hype and weeks of exhibitions and days of counting down the hours, it's finally here.

It used to be that the reigning champions were the opening act. Thus Argentina, the best team in the world, with Diego Maradona, the best player in the world, kicked off the 1990 tournament in Milan against Cameroon.

It was the moment when African soccer arrived. From a boycott in 1966 to defeating the defending title holders in twenty-four years, the transformation was remarkable. The Dark Continent's countries were never written off again.

In 1978, Tunisia were the first Africans to win a game at the finals, in 1982 Algeria beat West Germany, in 1986 Morocco became the first African nation to reach the knockout stage. But no one—really, no one—knew anything about 500–1 outsiders Cameroon. The extent of our knowledge was that four starters plied their trade in the French lower leagues.

Quickly it was obvious they were not overawed by the occasion. Within the opening 10 minutes Benjamin Massing was booked, they threw themselves into robust challenges all over the field, stopping (by fair means and foul) the South Americans from getting into a rhythm. At halftime, Argentinean coach Carlos

Cameroon's Omam Biyik shocks the world with his winning goal against Argentina in the opening match at the 1990 World Cup in the San Siro, Milan.

Bilardo brought on Claudio Caniggia to add his electric pace to the attack. The Argentineans improved, Maradona dropped deeper to orchestrate the play, but still they couldn't force the breakthrough.

With an hour gone, André Kana-Biyik was sent off for a trip on Caniggia. But his brother, François Omam-Biyik, ensured it didn't matter. Shortly afterwards he rose like a salmon to head a free kick, and it slipped under goalkeeper Nery Pumpido and into the goal. The Africans were ahead.

With two minutes remaining, and in the throes of ever-more desperate defending, Caniggia evaded a couple of tackles before being scythed down by Massing. It's one of those indelible World Cup images, Caniggia, flying with his long blond hair blowing in the wind, bent almost double as he fights to stay on his feet. He is tackled once, tackled twice, before succumbing to the third to end up dumped in a heap by the reckless, dangerous challenge that ended with Massing's cleat flying across the field and another dismissal.

But Cameroon held on. The champions had been defeated by a team from west Africa with nine men. They went on to become the first Africans to reach the quarterfinal.

Twelve years later, the holders France were beaten, 1–0, by Senegal in the opening game. But twenty-one out of the twenty-three in their squad were based in Europe and sixteen played in the French top-flight. "No team could ever again do what we did in 1990," said Cameroon's hip-shimmying forward Roger Milla. "The element of surprise is not there."

# 2002, Second Round
**South Korea 2, Italy 1**
**Quarterfinal**
**South Korea 0, Spain 0 (South Korea win 5–3 on penalties)**

If 1990 was when the Africans grew up, 2002 was when the Asians came of age. South Korea rolled all the way to the semifinal, though their success was coated in controversy.

They dispatched a pair of European giants on their fairytale run, but the co-hosts benefited from two generously refereed contests. When a top dog is humbled by a pup the loser often whines foul. South Koreans say their limited but hardworking unit deserved both victories, even if they got the rub of the green with a couple of key calls. Both Latin countries allege it was a plot to prolong the host's World Cup participation. Whatever the case, the Koreans did benefit from some strange officiating.

The Italians' defeat to North Korea in 1966 was highlighted when the teams took the field, thousands of home supporters holding up cards spelling out, "Again 1966," in the hope of picking at that particular psychological scar. Within five minutes, the Koreans won a penalty, but it was saved by Gigi Buffon, the most expensive goalkeeper in the world. Instead Italy took the lead through Christian Vieri, and as the contest progressed, the Koreans brought on attackers while Italy substituted in defenders. With just two minutes to play, Seol Ki-hyeon equalized: the Italians' negative and cautious tactics had backfired; South Korea deserved to draw level.

In extra time, Ecuadorian referee Byron Moreno cautioned Francesco Totti for diving when there had been contact with a Korean defender—it was his second yellow card and he was sent off. Then attacker Damiano Tommasi was pulled up wrongly for offside while clean through on goal. With three minutes to go, Ahn Jung-Hwan, who had missed the penalty, headed in the game-ending golden goal. He played in Italy for Perugia and was fired by his club. Like a hell-raising 1970s rock band, the enraged Italians smashed up their locker room (incidentally, referee Moreno was later suspended for 20 games in Ecuador after allowing 13 minutes of injury time during which a team scored twice to come from 3–2 down to win, 4–3. Then in 2010 he was arrested at New York's JFK airport for smuggling heroin and sentenced to two and a half years in jail).

Four days later the South Koreans did it again, beating Spain on penalties with Gamal Al-Ghandour from Egypt disallowed two (apparently) legitimate Spanish goals. The first, an own goal, was for an infringement no one else saw: despite repeated replays neither the commentators nor the viewers could identify the problem. Then what should have been a golden goal for Spain was chalked off when the linesman from Trinidad flagged that the ball had gone out of play in the buildup when it clearly had not.

Rather than a complex web of deceit, I think the blame lies with FIFA and their insistence on "rewarding" referees from minor soccer nations with prestigious jobs at their premier event (the other linesman was from Uganda). These games should be controlled by the very best officials on their list with weekly big-game experience, not part-time officials from the Caribbean. I am sure it was not a coincidence that two highly-experienced European referees took charge of the semifinals.

# 2010, Quarterfinal
## Uruguay 1, Ghana 1 (Uruguay win 4–2 on penalties)

Eighty years after lifting the first World Cup, Uruguay won this epic quarterfinal battle thanks to one man's decisive and divisive deed. To some he was a heroic player who sacrificed himself for his country, to others he was a despicable villain. Africa was close to having a nation in the last four of the tournament, but the hearts of a team representing more than a billion people were broken by one man, Ajax striker Luis Suárez.

The South Americans forced keeper Richard Kingson into three smart saves within the first half-an-hour of this match in Soccer City stadium, Johannesburg. But deep into first-half injury time, Ghana midfielder Sulley Muntari hit a bending shot from 40 yards that flew into the net to give the Africans an unlikely lead. In the second half, Atlético Madrid's Diego Forlán curled in a free-kick to level the score, and a combination of excellent keeping and poor finishing meant it remained deadlocked at 90 minutes.

You sensed Uruguay wilting in the heat and it was the Africans who carved out the better opportunities. In injury time Ghana sent a last-gasp free kick into the box, the ball bounced to Stephen Appiah, whose shot was blocked by Suarez defending on the goal-line, the rebound ballooned up to Dominic Adiyiah, his header was about to cross the line, Suárez batted the ball away with his hand. Suárez was sent off and the last kick of the game would be a penalty to Ghana. Asamoah Gyan stepped up to score from 12 yards and make history.

He hit the bar.

The match went to penalties instead.

Moments later, Gyan showed incredible courage to score Ghana's first kick in the shootout, but Adiyiah missed and Sebastian Abreu's cheeky chip straight down the center put the South Americans into the semis for the first time in forty years.

Suárez's teammates, coach, and country hailed him as the selfless savior of their World Cup dream. He was unrepentant, saying it was an instinctive reaction and calling it, "the save of the tournament." Referencing Maradona's similar antics in 1986 he claimed it was, "the real 'Hand of God.'"

The Ghana team and their Serbian coach Milovan Rajevac were distraught. They had been given a gilt-edged chance to reach the last four and were a goal-line handball away from creating history.

## 2014, Semifinal
### Germany 7, Brazil 1

We end with the most incredible, unbelievable, unexpected, result of all.

The hosts and favorites, the most successful country in the tournament's history, humbled beyond belief. The Germans rattled in a recordbreaking four goals in six minutes and were 5–0 up at halftime. The only other countries in World Cup history to go in 5–0 behind at the break were Zaire and Haiti. Apparently in the locker room the Germans countenanced against scoring too many more in the second half so they wouldn't embarrass their opponents. Too late.

Records tumbled on a tumultuous evening in Belo Horizonte, scene of that other great upset when the USA had beaten England sixty-four years previously.

The worst loss ever by a host country. The largest winning margin in a semifinal or final. The most goals (equal with Switzerland in 1954) conceded by a host in one match. Brazil's first World Cup semifinal defeat since 1938. In a couple of ironic twists, Germany overtook Brazil as the country to have scored most goals in the tournament's history, 223 compared with 221.

And the victory secured their eighth appearance in a final— nudging them ahead of Brazil's seven.

Germany netted as many goals in 68 minutes as they had in their previous six semifinals combined. Brazil's worst-ever home loss. Their greatest margin of defeat ever (equaling a 6–0 reverse by Uruguay in 1920). The end of their 62-match unbeaten run in home competitive matches stretching back *almost 40 years* to 1975. The first time they had conceded five goals or more since that 6–5 win against Poland in 1938.

Beforehand it had been too close to call between the nations ranked second and third in the world. I have never watched a match with the same degree of bewilderment. For those astonishing six minutes the Germans ran riot, a blitzkrieg of attacking force that shredded the Brazilian defense. For 300 seconds it was a marauding wave of white that found their target every single time they ventured forward. At the end of the 90 minutes the Germans had scored seven times from only 10 shots on target. Eviscerating effective efficiency.

Thomas Müller opened the scoring in the 11th minute but it was that mental spell halfway through the first half that ran the hosts ragged: Miroslav Klose doubled the lead; Toni Kroos added a third; from the kickoff, he dispossessed Fernandinho and finished the move to make it 4–0; Sami Khedira hit another in the 29th minute. Inside half-an-hour, the shellshocked Samba Boys were 5–0 behind, the formation crumbling, the defense parting like the Red Sea on repeat mode.

Substitute André Schürrle scored twice in the space of 10 minutes to make it 7–0 before Oscar hit the most meaningless consolation goal ever in injury time. Brazilian coach Luiz Felipe "Big Phil" Scolari resigned. His German counterpart Joachim Löw played down the result and declared, "We didn't celebrate. We were happy, but we still have a job to do."

They completed the job and beat Argentina in the final. Of course they did.

# CHAPTER SEVEN

# THE CONTENDERS

At 9 p.m. on Tuesday, November 15, 2017, I drove four blocks from the art gallery where I teach fiction writing to Finn McCool's Irish Pub in Mid-City, New Orleans. I wanted to catch the second half of the second leg of the intercontinental playoff between New Zealand and Peru, the battle to win the 32nd, and final, spot at the 2018 World Cup.

The South Americans led, 1–0, at the break, but an equalizer by the Kiwis would put them through on the away goals rule. I was rooting for them as I know their coach Anthony Hudson (we met when he played briefly in the Big Easy), but it was the home nation who scored to seal a 2–0 victory.

It felt anticlimatic and I experienced a sense of melancholy at the low-key ending to a sprawling, meandering qualification process that had featured more than 200 countries and encompassed all six inhabited continents. It had started with Timor-Leste's 4–1 victory over Mongolia in Dili on March 12, 2015, and after more than 800 matches it ended with delirious celebrating home fans in Lima, 979 days later.

Peru may have made the tournament, but there will be some notable absentees when it kicks off on June 14 in Russia. Missing their first competition in more than thirty years, of course, are the USA. Just as shocking, four-time winners Italy failed to make it for only the second time in history, a failure that sent the soccer-crazy nation into meltdown with newspapers running headlines like "Apocalypse Now!"

Chile may be the reigning Copa America champions but they are also staying at home. In Africa, Cameroon had qualified for six out of the last seven World Cups but won't be at this one. Holland were third at the last tournament in Brazil and are three-time finalists, but their players will be spending the summer on the beach too. And my home nation Northern Ireland were devastated by an egregious penalty decision in their playoff against Switzerland that ultimately proved decisive.

Enough about who is missing. Who is going? The usual suspects: defending champions and favorites Germany, challengers France and Spain from Europe, South American big hitters Brazil and Argentina. Can Portugal repeat their success at the 2016 European Championship, are Belgium's embarrassment of riches capable of winning the trophy, will new boys Iceland or Panama knock out a big gun? Let's take a look at the thirty-two teams competing at sports' greatest event:

# GROUP A

## RUSSIA

British Prime Minister Sir Winston Churchill called Russia, "a riddle, wrapped in a mystery, inside an enigma." Almost eighty years later it could describe their soccer team.

Sometimes it seems like they just don't care. They were bounced out in the group stage at both the last World Cup and the Euros, and in recent friendlies they conceded four goals to Costa Rica and were well beaten by the Czech Republic.

In their three finals appearances as an independent nation since the breakup of the Soviet Union they are yet to get past the first round. The South Africans are the only hosts who never made the knockout stage. With years to prepare, an easier draw as a top seed, and playing at home, for the Russians to emulate this "achievement" would be an unthinkable national disaster.

# SAUDI ARABIA

The lowest-ranked country at the finals, just making it there was a major achievement for the nation who barely scrapped into the top 100 when the qualifying cycle kicked off. A surprise package in 1994 when they made the second round, they have failed to win a match in their three subsequent appearances and have been missing since 2006.

Days after qualifying, the Green Falcons recruited Argentinean coach Edgardo Bauza, but he was then fired after only five games. They appointed his fellow national Juan Antonio Pizzi who had resigned from his post with Chile. What effect this South American coaching merry-go-round has on the team, we will find out come June.

# EGYPT

Despite being one of the largest countries on the continent, and winning the African Cup of Nations seven times, the Pharaohs had not made the World Cup since 1990—indeed four of those continental titles have come since they last made the tournament. But after a period of civil unrest and national upheaval, the team finally found their consistency and qualified with a game to spare at the expense of perennial American opponents Ghana. Now under the expert guidance of veteran Argentinean coach Héctor Cúper, they will be aiming to escape the group stage for the first time on their third appearance at the finals.

## URUGUAY

Uruguay finished second in a close-fought CONMEBOL qualifying but only guaranteed their slot on the final matchday, meaning coach Óscar Washington Tábarez will be in charge of his homeland for an impressive fourth World Cup. If they are to emulate their fourth place in 2010 they will again be calling on Luis Suárez, the player whose goal-line clearance with his arm got them to the semifinal.

Controversial and mercurial, he is a predatory finisher level with Lionel Messi at the top of the all-time South American qualifying goalscoring chart with 21. Should his attacking prowess be rendered temporarily toothless (sorry), then his strike partner Edinson Cavani, tearing up the French league with Paris Saint-Germain, can bring bite to the attack (sorry again). It was their goals that ended La Celeste's run of four consecutive fifth-place finishes in the region's preliminaries.

# GROUP B

## PORTUGAL

Portugal finally won a major international trophy with their success at Euro 2016. In 1966 they made the World Cup semifinal, the Golden Generation of the early twenty-first century ended with a dulled legacy, but this team triumphed where their predecessors had failed and shook off the label "chronic underachievers." They have now qualified for eight straight World Cups or European Championships.

True, they are built around one man. But what a man—the supreme, sublime, skillful Cristiano Ronaldo. They won nine out of ten qualifiers, and it's no coincidence their solitary defeat came in a game he missed. With a fit Ronaldo in full-attack, free-flowing form, they will be confident of beating anyone.

## SPAIN

To misquote Mark Twain, rumors of Spain's demise have been greatly exaggerated. When the reigning champions were humiliated, 5–1, by Holland in 2014, it was seen as signaling the death knell for tiki-taka soccer and as heralding the dismantling of the Spaniard squad that had conquered the world. Not quite.

No team built on players from Barcelona and Real Madrid is going to struggle for long. This is a collection who regularly compete in the latter stages of the Champions League, who would saunter onto nearly every national team on earth, but who may not even make the bench for the Red Fury. They will be desperate to make up for crashing out so early last time, and a motivated and disciplined Spanish side will make for a fearsome opponent.

## MOROCCO

The Atlas Lions made it to three out of four World Cups between 1986 and 1998 at a time when it was harder to qualify from Africa as the continent had a smaller representation. Russia sees them return to the tournament after an absence of two decades, and although they have continued to produce exciting players, they have lacked strength in depth. Now infused with a new wave of young European-based talent, they edged out the Ivory Coast for a finals spot. Defensively resilient, it remains to be seen if the current crop of youth will have enough experience to find their way to goal.

## IRAN

This is Iran's fifth World Cup but so far they have managed to score just seven goals and record a solitary victory—a 2–1 win against the USA in 1998. They were the first Asians to book a place in Russia and negotiated eighteen preliminary matches without defeat. Their level of competition (in the first stage their nearest challengers were Oman and Turkmenistan) will mean their fellow finalists are not trembling at the thought of being pitched in with the Persians, but their qualification campaign made history as they became the first country to record 12 consecutive shutouts, a stretch lasting almost 19 hours.

You can guarantee they will be well-organized and prepared thanks to their boss: Carlos Queiroz's credentials are impeccable as he has worked at both Manchester United and Real Madrid, and he won the Under-20 world title twice with his native Portugal.

# GROUP C

## FRANCE

Which French incarnation will we see in Russia? A swashbuckling squad that picks apart opponents with a nonchalant Gallic shrug, or a collection of individuals on a roster racked with backstabbing and infighting? They won a tough qualifying group

France is hoping that midfielder Paul Pogba, seen here in a qualifier against Holland, will reproduce his club form for Manchester United while playing with the national team in Russia.

featuring Sweden, Holland, and Bulgaria, and as an illustration of how highly the current crop of Les Blues are rated consider this: three of the most expensive transfers of all time involve Frenchmen. Kylian Mbappe's move from Monaco to Paris Saint-Germain could end up costing close to €200 million ($240 million) with add-ons, Ousmané Dembelé went from Borussia Dortmund to Barcelona for a fee that could climb as high as €150m ($180m), while Paul Pogba rejoined Manchester United from Juventus for more than €100m ($120m). They have the capability to improve on their quarterfinal exit in Brazil—the more pertinent question is, do they have the temperament?

## AUSTRALIA

The Aussies' gamble to switch regions and play qualifiers in the Asian zone has paid off, and another two-legged intercontinental victory means they are at their fourth World Cup in a row. Previously the Socceroos were often dominated by a few big names who plied their trade in England, but most of the current squad is home-based as the domestic soccer scene Down Under has mushroomed. Having won the Asian Cup and successfully negotiated playoff victories against Syria and Honduras—a pair of countries and climates as opposite as you can get—on the way to Russia, they have added experience and assurance to their team DNA.

## PERU

Peru's playoff victory over New Zealand ended their thirty-six-year World Cup drought. Although they lost home and away to Chile, they squeaked in ahead of the Copa America champions on goal difference: both finished on 26 points, but Peru scored 27 goals and conceded 26, while Chile scored 26 and conceded 27. Ironically, their fates were sealed by Bolivia fielding an ineligible player in their win over Peru and their tie with Chile. FIFA expunged the results and awarded 3–0 wins to their opponents— if that had not happened then Chile would have finished a point higher than Peru and taken their place in the decider against the All Whites. It is Peru's fourth tournament; they are unlikely to repeat 1970's run to the quarterfinals.

## DENMARK

The Danes were the seeds everyone wanted to draw in the European playoffs, but anyone who thought they were weak was laboring under a misapprehension. They had already beaten a handy Poland outfit, 4–0, in qualifying so they boast some serious firepower, and they steamrollered, then demolished, and finally embarrassed the Republic of Ireland, 5–1, in Dublin. Creative force Christian Eriksen is their most skillful and important player as his hat trick against the Irish proved, while at the other end Kasper Schmeichel is the trustworthy custodian. He will want to excel at the World Cup twenty years after his legendary goalkeeper father Peter helped Denmark to the quarterfinal.

# GROUP D

## ARGENTINA

It's Joan Crawford and Bette Davis, Ozzy Osbourne or Alice Cooper. Whether you prefer Lionel Messi or Cristiano Ronaldo doesn't matter—the diminutive Argentinean is one of the greatest talents the world has ever seen.

Like Maradona a generation ago, he is Atlas carrying the weight and fate of La Albiceleste on his shoulders. When his country cried out for a savior, Messi was their Messiah. They had not won in four games going into the final showdown with Ecuador, a horrible run that included a defeat to Bolivia and a home tie with Venezuela. Needing victory to book their spot at the finals, they went 1–0 down within seconds of kickoff. Messi singlehandedly hauled Argentina to Russia with an outrageous hat trick. If they are to make their sixth World Cup final, he needs his supporting cast to show up.

# ICELAND

And we thought their pillaging raid at Euro 2016 was a flash in the pan. With a population of fewer than 350,000, they have made history as the smallest country to make the tournament, a quarter of the size of the previous record holder Trinidad and Tobago (the USA failed to make the finals despite having 1,000 times as many citizens to call upon). The North Atlantic islanders finished top of a section containing Croatia, Ukraine, and Turkey.

For the 2010 World Cup, they languished last in their qualification group, by 2016 they were beating England in the knockout stage of the Euros. They often set up in an adventurous formation with two out-and-out attackers, a rarity in today's world of cautious international soccer, and these Viking marauders will be on a mission to prove that small is beautiful.

# CROATIA

The Croats blow hot and cold. I watched them from a fourth-row seat at Euro 2016 as they raced into a 2–0 lead against the Czech Republic, but they managed to let that lead slip and ended up with a 2–2 tie in a contest they controlled. That 90-minute snapshot encapsulates the Balkan nation. Their Spanish-based pair of playmakers, Real Madrid's Luka Modrić and Barcelona's Ivan Rakitić, supply the ammunition for the duo who play in Italy, Ivan Perišić from Inter and Mario Mandžukić at Juventus. With an attacking quartet like that, Croatia should have had more success than their one semifinal appearance that came in 1998 at their inaugural tournament as an independent country.

# NIGERIA

The Nigerians are usually Africa's best bet for a World Cup berth. This is their sixth appearance in the last seven finals, and despite drawing both Cameroon and Algeria in qualifying they were still the first nation from the continent to cement a spot at Russia.

They typically perform admirably, if not spectacularly, and will be motivated to reach the quarterfinals for the first time. It's a squad blessed with stamina and lightning bursts of pace, and with stars like Chelsea's Victor Moses and Alex Iwobi from Arsenal they can add top-level experience to their superb athleticism. German coach Gernot Rohr will be confident the Super Eagles can live up to their nickname.

# GROUP E

## BRAZIL

If ever a country had something to prove at a World Cup, it is Brazil this time around after their humiliation by Germany in 2014. If their form in qualifying is anything to go by they are determined to reclaim their position on the winners' podium. They were beaten by Chile in the first game in October 2015, but since then they have lost just one competitive match (when they exited the Copa America group stage for the first time ever), and set a South American record by winning nine successive World Cup preliminaries.

Neymar, seen here scoring for Brazil against Chile in a South American preliminary match, became the most expensive soccer player in the world with his transfer between Barcelona and Paris Saint-Germain for more than $260m in 2017.

In defense, Dani Alves and Marcelo are perhaps the world's best fullback pair, in attack Neymar, Gabriel Jesus, and Philippe Coutinho form a tantalizing and terrifying trio. They were the first country to make it to Russia—they will expect to be the last to leave.

## SWITZERLAND

The team that broke my heart with a playoff win against my home nation Northern Ireland. FIFA has been bedeviled by scandal, and it was the country where the organization is housed that was awarded a scandalous penalty kick, the ball striking the Irish defender on the back of his shoulder rather than his arm. The successful conversion was the only thing separating the Swiss and Irish over two legs. It's still a bitter pill to swallow for us Ulstermen.

Switzerland won nine out of ten qualifiers but finished behind Portugal on goal difference. This is their fourth successive trip to the finals, and their 11th overall, but they haven't made it as far as the last eight since they hosted in 1954. Excuse me for hoping that when they exit this go around, they are victims of a cruel and baffling refereeing decision.

## COSTA RICA

The Ticos were written off at the last World Cup after drawing three former winners (Uruguay, Italy, and England) in the first round, but they won the group undefeated and then squeezed past Greece to make the last eight. They almost went all the way to the semifinal, only losing on penalties to Holland. It's unlikely, however, lightning will strike twice.

They qualified with ease and chalked up deserved home and away victories over the USA. Compact in defense and expansive in attack, they did, though, fail to win any of their last three matches: whether it was a team coasting home after doing the hard work, or the sign of an outfit who has lost momentum, we will find out in Russia.

## SERBIA

Serbia topped a hard-fought qualifying section in which just six points separated four countries. Their players have names that look like a collection of spilled Scrabble letters, but they are seasoned, consistent, technically-gifted performers for top European clubs.

It feels like you need an atlas, a history lesson, a geography course and a degree in politics to follow the Serbs' participation at the World Cup. First they were Yugoslavia, then they became Serbia and Montenegro, and now they are making their second trip to the finals as an independent nation. They will be hoping to get further than their first-round exit in 2010.

# GROUP F

## GERMANY

I think they will join Brazil on five World Cup wins. Teams can have a bad day, key players can get injured, a misfiring attack can fail to score, an individual error can be costly. But I don't think there are twenty-three players more talented or better prepared than the Germans.

I saw them at close quarters twice against Northern Ireland in the space of fifteen months. The results of 1–0 and 3–1 suggest close games but don't tell the whole story. Germany were dominant, the speed of their passing and the fluidity of their attacks staggering.

Their goal difference of 39 was a European qualifying record and they won all ten games to be the only nation from any confederation to make it to the tournament with a perfect record. I believe they will be the first country to retain the trophy since Brazil in 1962, more than half a century ago.

# MEXICO

They strolled into the World Cup with three matches left to notch up their seventh straight finals appearance. Their only defeat in the preliminaries was their final contest against Honduras—which meant the USA would be staying at home. With that loss, the country some Americans want to isolate with a wall, condemned them to a summer of isolation.

This will be El Tri's sixteenth trip to the finals and only the heavyweight trio Brazil, Italy, and Argentina has been there more often. But inevitably, they finish as runners-up in the group stage and go out in the first knockout round. Their coach is former Colombian international Juan Carlos Osorio, who had a spell in MLS in charge of Chicago Fire, then led the New York Red Bulls for two years. So at least America can claim a tenuous presence at the tournament.

# SWEDEN

Italy was the country everyone wanted to avoid in the European playoffs so Sweden were written off when they drew them, especially as they had to play the second leg away from home. But the

Scandinavians fully earned their World Cup spot by recording two shutouts against the Azzurri—it is only the second time the Italians have failed to qualify for the tournament. The Swedes finished behind the classy French and above Holland in the preliminaries as they return to the finals after missing out in both 2010 and 2014. They are lacking the star power of previous years, but with a resolute back line their forwards are capable of carving out an opening to nick a goal—if you don't believe me, just ask the Italians.

## SOUTH KOREA

The most successful Asian nation has been to every tournament for the last thirty-two years. Their nine-in-a-row record is unmatched outside of Europe and South America, although this time the Taeguk Warriors were run close by underdogs Syria and lost three matches in the final qualifying group.

Their exports are increasingly making an impact in Europe's top leagues and forward Son Heung-min is the most expensive Asian player ever. He was signed by Bayer Leverkusen for a club record €10 million ($12m) in 2013, then transferred to Tottenham for £22 million ($30m) and is the top Asian scorer in Premier League history. Unusually for an Asian country, they are not led by a foreigner but are coached by Shin Tae-yong.

# GROUP G

## BELGIUM

Belgium won a weak qualifying section, with Greece and Bosnia and Herzegovina providing the competition (that's two countries by the way, not three), but would a different group have made any difference? Look at the Red Devils' lineup: Eden Hazard of Chelsea has arguably been the Premier League's best player over the past few seasons; in goal his club teammate Thibaut Courtois is as talented as he is lanky. Kevin De Bruyne has been outstanding for Manchester City, Romelu Lukaku cost Manchester United more than $90 million last year, they have Thomas Vermaelen and Moussa Dembélé and Jan Vertonghen and Michy Batshuayi and Marouane Fellaini and Vincent Kompany and . . . you get the picture.

A squad stuffed with skill and experience will be intent on improving on their 2014 performance when they lost to Argentina in the last eight. With Hazard bearing down one wing and De Bruyne tearing things up on the other, they are one of the competition's dark horses.

## PANAMA

In the hexagonal they scored only nine goals (the USA hit 17), won just three games, and went six successive matches without a win. The first time they occupied an automatic qualification slot was in the dying embers of the campaign when Roman Torres hit a late winner against Costa Rica. It may have meant heartache for the USA, but you can't deny the unheralded Central Americans their moment in the sun.

In 2014 it was the Canal Men who suffered last-gasp agony. In the final preliminary for Brazil they were leading an already-qualified USA, 2–1, in injury time, a score that would have put them in the intercontinental playoff, but two stoppage-time goals from the Americans robbed them off fourth spot. It took them four years, but they finally got to banish the pain.

# TUNISIA

The Carthage Eagles were once a familiar sight at the World Cup, qualifying for three successive tournaments between 1998 and 2006, but like their neighbors Morocco they too have struggled recently. They had a nervy conclusion to their preliminary campaign: needing only one point from their final home game with already-eliminated Libya, they scrapped into Russia with an uninspiring, apprehensive scoreless tie. In their twelve matches in the competition they have scored eight goals and recorded just a single win, though that 3–1 victory in 1978 against Mexico was the first ever achieved at the finals by an African nation. Forty years later they will need to repeat that feat if they are to reach the knockout rounds.

# ENGLAND

Ah, the good old Three Lions. You know the story by now: they ease through qualifying, ease out of the group stage, ease past a Paraguay or a Sweden in round two, get knocked out on penalties in the quarterfinals by Germany or Argentina. Is there any chance we will read a different script this time?

Probably not. The current crop of Englishmen generally lack invention and are overshadowed by the dazzling imports who light up the Premier League weekly, although the exception is Harry Kane who has carried his phenomenal goal scoring over to his country from his club Tottenham. However, time is on their side, and this young roster should improve on their first-round exit in 2014.

# GROUP H

## POLAND

No one scored more goals in qualifying than Robert Lewand-owski. The Bayern Munich marksman hit 16 in just 10 matches and set a new European record, his haul impressive for not being artificially inflated with a hatful against the likes of San Marino or Gibraltar. At twenty-nine and the peak of his physical prowess, the deadly striker will be a handful for any defense.

After a run of four successive World Cups in the '70s and '80s, the Poles have been absent for twelve years. But they were impressive at Euro 2016 and in qualifying, and their partisan fans will enjoy the chance to invade Russia this summer.

## SENEGAL

After a bye in the first qualifying round, the Senegalese beat the island of Madagascar, most famous for the home of the extinct dodo, to make it to the final stage. Burkina Faso and the Cape Verde Islands were then their nearest challengers. That was their route to Russia: the soccer gods may as well have sat them on golf carts and strewn rose petals in their path. Unsurprisingly, they went unbeaten in eight matches, but the Lions of Teranga will find it much tougher at the finals. It is only their second visit to the tournament after their gate-crashing, giant-killing debut in 2002 when they defeated the holders France and made it to the quarterfinal, losing to Turkey on a golden goal.

## COLOMBIA

The Colombians stumbled over the finishing line, failing to win any of their last four games but sneaking into the final qualification slot when Chile lost three of their final four matches. They have chalked up five previous tournaments, their best showing in 2014 when they beat fellow South Americans Uruguay then narrowly lost to hosts Brazil in the last eight. That success was in large part due to talismanic striker James Rodríguez whose six goals in five contests won him the Golden Boot and a near $100m transfer from Monaco to Real Madrid. Despite a healthy 36 goals in 110 games for the Spanish club, he has since been farmed out on loan to Bayern Munich in Germany.

## JAPAN

This may be Japan's sixth successive World Cup, but it's unlikely they will improve on their best-ever performance of getting to the second round, something they have only achieved once outside their own country. Always referred to as workmanlike and industrious, it's a fair criticism to accuse them of missing flair and creativity. But hard work and discipline are admirable qualities to build on, and their record in qualifying proves they know their way to the goal. Expect them to rely heavily on playmaker Keisuke Honda who now plays in Mexico, though for years his displays for Italian giants AC Milan had him linked with many big European clubs.

# AFTERWORD

So no USA at the World Cup ending the run of seven successive tournaments. If you are younger than thirty-two it's the first time it's happened in your life. Which country do you support instead?

Also missing are the cool kids of Italy, Holland, Chile—and Northern Ireland because of our criminal playoff defeat to Switzerland and a ridiculous penalty kick award. Let's move on swiftly, the bile and bitterness is rising in my stomach.

Many Americans will adopt a team and most will probably delve into their family history. They will get behind the old country from whence their ancestors embarked on a journey to a place that once welcomed "huddled masses, yearning to breathe free," instead of building a border barrier to keep them out and placing them on no-fly lists.

Maybe your descendants sailed across on the Mayflower and it's jolly old England for you, the Revolutionary War viewed as a petty embarrassing family squabble that only gets mentioned when Great Aunt Mary hits the sherry on July 4. Perhaps your grandparents were Eastern European emigrants granted citizenship after World War II, thus you will be cheering on Poland. Or you will be throwing your weight behind Peru simply because you once petted a llama.

If you want to jump on a bandwagon while simultaneously getting with a winning team, go for Germany or Brazil. If picking one of the favorites with the best players on the planet feels restrictive, add in France or Spain.

If you don't want to follow a nation from that quartet, but you can't throw away your bet on a rank outsider, compromise and go for, if not exactly a dark horse, at least a slightly tanned one. Belgium or Argentina are your choices here. If one of these six do not win the World Cup, then I should fly everyone reading this to Qatar for the next tournament in 2022.

I understand that in America winning is everything and second is just best loser, but there are options if your ambition is limited to being aligned with a bunch of fans in the pub three days this summer. To back a wee plucky underdog, buy an Iceland scarf or a Panama hat. To grab a kiss from an attractive statuesque blond or blonde, support Sweden or Denmark. If you intend to drink a lot, learn new toasts, and make inroads into deciphering the Cyrillic alphabet, root for Russia. If you intend to drink a lot, learn new toasts, and make inroads into deciphering the Antipodean accent, root for Australia.

Wrap yourself in a flag of convenience and pick a country to support. I hope you have fun. Just promise me you won't support the Swiss . . .

# SCHEDULE

## Group A

Russia
Uruguay
Egypt
Saudi Arabia

June 14, Moscow
Russia vs. Saudi Arabia

June 15, Ekaterinburg
Egypt vs. Uruguay

June 19, Saint Petersburg
Russia vs. Egypt

June 20, Rostov-on-Don
Uruguay vs. Saudi Arabia

June 25, Samara
Uruguay vs. Russia

June 25, Volgograd
Saudi Arabia vs. Egypt

## Group B

Portugal
Spain
Iran
Morocco

June 15, Sochi
Portugal vs. Spain

June 15, Saint Petersburg
Morocco vs. Iran

June 20, Moscow
Portugal vs. Morocco

June 20, Kazan
Iran vs. Spain

June 25, Saransk
Iran vs. Portugal

June 25, Kaliningrad
Spain vs. Morocco

## Group C

France
Peru
Denmark
Australia

June 16, Kazan
France vs. Australia

June 16, Saransk
Peru vs. Denmark

June 21, Ekaterinburg
France vs. Peru

June 21, Samara
Denmark vs. Australia

June 26, Moscow
Denmark vs. France

June 26, Sochi
Australia vs. Peru

## Group D

Argentina
Croatia
Iceland
Nigeria

June 16, Moscow
Argentina vs. Iceland

June 16, Kaliningrad
Croatia vs. Nigeria

June 21, Nizhny Novgorod
Argentina vs. Croatia

June 22, Volgograd
Nigeria vs. Iceland

June 26, Saint Petersburg
Nigeria vs. Argentina

June 26, Rostov-on-Don
Iceland vs. Croatia

## Group E

Brazil
Switzerland
Costa Rica
Serbia

June 17, Rostov-on-Don
Brazil vs. Switzerland

June 17, Samara
Costa Rica vs. Serbia

June 22, Saint Petersburg
Brazil vs. Costa Rica

June 22, Kaliningrad
Serbia vs. Switzerland

June 27, Moscow
Serbia vs. Brazil

June 27, Nizhny Novgorod
Switzerland vs. Costa Rica

## Group F

Germany
Mexico
Sweden
South Korea

June 17, Moscow
Germany vs. Mexico

June 18, Nizhny Novgorod
Sweden vs. South Korea

June 23, Sochi
Germany vs. Sweden

June 23, Rostov-on-Don
South Korea vs. Mexico

June 27, Kazan
South Korea vs. Germany

June 27, Ekaterinburg
Mexico vs. Sweden

## Group G

Belgium
England
Tunisia
Panama

June 18, Sochi
Belgium vs. Panama

June 18, Volgograd
Tunisia vs. England

June 23, Moscow
Belgium vs. Tunisia

June 24, Nizhny Novgorod
England vs. Panama

June 28, Kaliningrad
England vs. Belgium

June 28, Saransk
Panama vs. Tunisia

**Group H**

Poland
Colombia
Senegal
Japan

June 19, Moscow
Poland vs. Senegal

June 19, Saransk
Colombia vs. Japan

June 24, Kazan
Poland vs. Colombia

June 24, Ekaterinburg
Japan vs. Senegal

June 28, Volgograd
Japan vs. Poland

June 28, Samara
Senegal vs. Colombia

Round of 16

June 30, Sochi
1A vs. 2B

June 30, Kazan
1C vs. 2D

July 1, Moscow
1B vs. 2A

July 1, Nizhny Novgorod
1D vs. 2C

July 2, Samara
1E vs. 2F

July 2, Rostov-on-Don
1G vs. 2H

July 3, Saint Petersburg
1F vs. 2E

July 3, Moscow
1H vs. 2G

*Quarterfinals*

July 6, Nizhny Novgorod
1A/2B vs. 1C/2D

July 6, Kazan
1E/2F vs. 1G/2H

July 7, Sochi
1B/2A vs. 1D/2C

July 7, Samara
1F/2E vs. 1H/2G

*Semifinals*

July 10, Saint Petersburg
1A/2B/1C/2D vs.
1E/2F/1G/2H

July 11, Moscow
1F/2E/1H/2G vs.
1B/2A/1D/2C

*Third-Place Match*

July 14, Saint Petersburg

*Final*

July 15, Moscow

# ACKNOWLEDGMENTS

Planning, researching, and writing a book based on almost 100 years of World Cup history is a lonely endeavor. Thankfully, many people enriched and enlivened my hours at the computer with their help, friendship, and love.

To Bill Wolfsthal and Ken Samelson at Skyhorse, thanks for your input, advice, and unrelenting patience with this Irish eejit.

To my family: Nicola, mum Linda, dad Billy, Carol and Jim, Tavares, Sandra, Anne, William, and Rachel. To Julie: We held on through a physical hurricane then a metaphorical one. We tried hard.

To those who sheltered and supported me in New Orleans and beyond: Neil and Rachael Billingham; Cat and Will Bishop; Paul and Gena Daley; Gurbir Dhillon; Sam and Joe Guichet; Benjamin and Shawn Haswell; Jonathan Hird; Jonathon Holmes; Carmel and Sean Kennedy; Patrick and Brenda Mitchell; Kevin and Erin Muggivan; Stephen and Pauline Patterson; Tom and Patricia Schoenbrun; Steve and Rachel Scully; Ian Seymour; Gordon and Dawn Sheals; Bert and Mary Swafford; Tony Tomelden and Stephanie Coleman; Keith Willey. To my fairy godmother Lynn Seager-Putterford, and Paul Dale.

To my writing students: Petrina Amacker; Harry Bruns; Chaya Conrad; Samantha Frost; Matt Haines; Rachel Henderson; Marissa Hogan; Cathryn Jones; Catherine Levendis; Laura Michaud; Debbie Pesses; Anne Reed; Ashley Rouen; Bill Tice, and Ginger Vehaskari. I learn more from you than you learn from me. But that's a low benchmark.

Finally, Elicia. You ruined me. But then you fixed me.